BURLESQUE RIVER
Book One

Kitty Bardot

www.BOROUGHSPUBLISHINGGROUP.com

PUBLISHER'S NOTE: This is a work of fiction. Names, characters, places and incidents either are the product of the author's imagination or are used fictitiously. Any resemblance to actual events, locales, business establishments or persons, living or dead, is coincidental. Boroughs Publishing Group does not have any control over and does not assume responsibility for author or third-party websites, blogs or critiques or their content.

BURLESQUE RIVER
Copyright © 2020 Kitty Bardot

ISBN: 978-1-951055-63-9

To my beautiful husband who inspires and encourages me in my every endeavor, no matter how wild it may seem. Also to my burlesque family, you know who you are!

ACKNOWLEDGMENTS

Special thanks to my brother A.E. Stueve for all the work he put in to helping me edit, and keeping my chin up during the search for a publisher.

BURLESQUE RIVER

Chapter One

"Can you see my vag?" Cindy calls to the small dressing room. Her wild purple afro is tamed under a black wig cap. She's adjusting her sequined merkin as the base of her multilayered costume. Five faces turn away from their mirrors toward her.

"Looks good from here," Bridgette responds, pulling a curler from her long, silken hair. It falls in a golden spiral to her shoulder.

"How 'bout you guys?" Cindy asks, turning to Amanda and Jessica sitting on the floor in front of a large mirror. "You've got a better angle." Jessica's thick, black ponytail swings as she turns fully around to get a better look.

"I don't see anything," she responds then perches back on her heels to get back to the task of meticulously painting her face.

"How 'bout you, Bunny?"

Amanda, who goes by Bunny, sitting on crossed legs, leans on her arms then lies flat. "I can see the back of your teeth," she shouts.

"I don't see anything. But, bitch, I can smell it," Calvin's velvet voice calls from behind Cindy. He looks back on his reflection and waves his hand in the air. His golden-brown eyes smile as he adds another coat of glitter to them.

"Fuck you, guys. This is serious. We've never been here before. And this town hasn't seen burlesque since the forties. We want to give them a good show. But not that good."

"You're fine, Cin." Amanda laughs as she sits up, returning to her makeup.

"Thank you," Cindy responds, crossing to stand behind her. "How are your curls?" she asks, pulling one out to check. "They need more time," she answers herself.

"Hey, Bunny." Lucy turns in her seat in front of another mirror, her long red hair falling like a mermaid's around her pale, bare shoulders. "What's this town like anyway? Doesn't seem as bumpkiny as you described it." She's fluttering her newly applied eyelashes with fingers in the corners to keep tears from ruining her eyeliner.

"This isn't my town. I grew up over the river. This is where you went when you were going to town. You know, where the action is."

"I bet you saw a lot of action here, didn't you, Bunny?" Jonathan enters through the curtains from the stage. He leans against a wall. His top hat hides his wild dark mane. A grizzled beard contradicts the vaudevillian cane he carries while the rest of his look comes from the free table at a garage sale. His pants are too short, jacket too big. Wrinkles adorn every garment.

Amanda cringes internally. "Nope," she says with a sigh. "I was a kid when I left. All starry-eyed, headed for the big city."

The past begins its whispers in her ear. For every memory she brushes away, another pops up. She sees the sagging old house exactly as she left it, her aunt scowling in the doorway.

"You ungrateful little slut." she shouted up the stairs as Amanda packed her backpack with the few possessions she had. "I don't know why I ever took you in," her aunt hissed as they crossed paths at the foot of the stairway. "No wonder your daddy didn't want you."

"I'm leaving, Betty. You don't have to worry about me anymore." Amanda had been working at the local gas station in town for a while, saving all her money. She could call a cab from there and take it into the city, but instead she'd buy a bus ticket for the first bus available. It didn't matter where.

"Bunny?" Jonathan called. She looks up at him. He looks concerned. In fact the whole room was looking at her, each beautifully painted pair of eyes watching her as she blinks away the tears that were sure to come. Calvin stretches his long, lean frame and crosses the room to hug her.

"Girl, I don't know where you went just now, but, stay away from there."

"For real, Bunny," Jessica says, patting Bunny on the knee.

"Thanks, guys. I'm all right. Bad memories is all. We get through tonight and it's back home to prepare for the biggest show of our lives."

"No kidding," Cindy says as she rifles through her bag for a pack of smokes. "Sucks we already had our tour scheduled when they called to book us."

"Yeah, but we couldn't miss this opportunity." Lucy steps beside Cindy, motioning for a cigarette. She pulls a second one out and hands it over. "Just think, a real theater. Not a bar with a stage, but a stage with lights, and dressing rooms, and a backstage. It's going to be awesome." Her husky voice trails off on daydreams.

"You're right," Cindy agrees. "Wish we had more time to prepare."

"We'll be fine," Calvin says, sauntering to his things for a smoke of his own. "Let's go see what there is to see." The three of them sweep through the curtain with Jonathan following close behind. Bridgette shakes her full head of curls out and sprays them heavily with hairspray.

"You sure you're all right, Amanda?" Her name doesn't sound right coming out of Bridgette's mouth. She always calls her Bunny, even off stage, even at home.

"Why'd you call me that? You never call me Amanda."

"I don't know. You don't seem like Bunny right now at all. You're somewhere else."

"She's right," Jessica agrees as she applies her mascara. "We lost you."

"I'm fine, guys, for real. It's been a long time since I've been this close to home. I know my aunt's dead and gone. Honestly, Amanda might as well be too, for all I care. I'm not the girl who left here. Not by a long shot."

"Well, it's only one night, then we're home."

"Yep," she agrees. "One night, then home."

***

Vic's standing behind the bar, counting the drawer, getting ready to open for the night. He's in one of his signature suits despite the heat. Polished and shining. The picture of a club owner. "Glad you made it out tonight. Was worried you were going to flake on me again," he says over his shoulder.

"Wouldn't miss it," Mike grunts out, carrying another case of bottles. He's chosen more casual attire, wearing a pair of jeans and a lightweight button-down.

"Yeah right," Vic scoffs. "When you gonna quit your day job anyway? I feel like I'm having all the fun here. I mean, what's the point of owning a club if you never spend any time in it?"

"I have fun." Mike's loading the bottles into the cooler two at a time.

"Sure thing, friend." Vic slides the drawer shut and turns to lean on the bar. "You know you wouldn't have come out tonight if I hadn't come to get you."

Mike shrugs. "I like my peace and quiet."

"You sound like my grandpa, man."

"I like your grandpa."

"What I'm saying is all work and no play makes Mike a dull boy."

"Hey, I'm here, aren't I? Not really interested in seeing a bunch of tattooed ladies with crazy-colored hair dance their daddy issues out on stage, but I'm here."

"You are." Vic pauses. "Remember all the plans we had for this place when we bought it? I have a good feeling that this is exactly the kind of thing we've been looking for. Something to really put us on the map. I've heard nothing but great things about this group."

"We'll see." There's a knock at the front door. Mike walks around to let the bartenders in. Moments later the first patrons arrive, and from that point on it's a constant flow of bodies through the door.

Mike and Vic stand, taking in the scene. Excited voices of a couple hundred people fill the small venue. With each drink consumed the din grows. Though the air conditioner is working its best, August sneaks its way in as bodies keep coming.

"Looks like we sold out," Vic says, rolling up the sleeves of his designer shirt. His tie is already loose at his neck. His jacket hangs on a hook behind him.

"Looks like," Mike responds, loosening another button on his shirt. "It's heating up in here."

"Yeah. Wait for the show. Had a chance to talk with the performers before you got here. They are some of the hottest chicks I've met."

"Really?" Mike asks, eyebrows raised.

Vic is in the habit of surrounding himself with beautiful women. Even the ladies tending bar are something to behold. Three of them are busy serving drinks currently. One, in fact, has a familiar face. Mike searches his mind for a name to attach to it. She smiles and blushes when their eyes meet. Her green eyes shine with a memory they share. "How ya been?" she asks as she mixes drinks.

"I'm good." He smiles, still searching for a name. She had been soft and yielding, he recalls, a bit drunk. But so was he. They'd stumbled through their night together. But he must have done something right. It'd been months. And here she is blushing and shining. Her body giving him all the clues that she'd like another round.

A man with an oversize top hat and ridiculous cane comes parading off the stage and through the scores of people taking their seats. He smiles and shakes their hands like a politician. His whole look reminds Mike of the Mad Hatter from *Alice in Wonderland*. Mike rolls his eyes to the embossed ceiling. *What am I getting myself into?* he thinks as the ragtag hobo approaches the bar.

"Vic." The guy smiles. "The girls are ready. We're waiting for the all clear."

"Give us a minute. Once the bar traffic slows down and everyone's in their seats."

"For sure. I'll look for the house lights to go down then." The guy nods to Mike with a step back.

"Jonathan," Vic calls before the guy turns to go. "I want you to meet my partner, Mike Nichols." Jonathan extends his hand. Mike shakes it as Vic says, "Jonathan Wayne, emcee for Burlesque A La Mode."

"Hope you're ready to be wildly entertained," Jonathan says with the flair of a magician and an easy laugh.

"I'm pretty hard to impress," Mike responds.

"I accept your challenge," Jonathan exclaims with a twirl of his cane. He turns and makes his way back through the throngs of people.

"Funny little guy," Mike says to Vic.

Vic laughs, nodding in agreement. Together they pitch in to help the bar staff get the rest of the crowd served and back to their seats. Vic gestures to Johnny Tuesday in the sound booth. The house lights drop. Stage lights go up. The crowd is hushed.

Ridiculous, and right on cue, Jonathan gallops from backstage with the clumsy grace of the most skilled comedian. "Ladies and gentlemen," he shouts. "Welcome to Burlesque A La Mode. I'm your host Jonathan Wayne." The crowd cheers.

"How many of you have seen a burlesque show before?" he inquires. A few hoots accompany polite applause. "Looks like you guys are in need of an education." He starts to dance and loosen his tie. "Bump, ba, ba, ba, bum, bum…" The crowd laughs. "Good, good. That's what I'm looking for. Your laughter makes me happy. Makes me want to do more so you laugh more. A's all around." He pauses, raising one finger in the air with a flourish. "That's not what these ladies want though. No, they are classy. They don't want your laughter. They are here for one thing and one thing only."

"Your money," someone shouts from a table near the front.

"Oh no, sir, they know I don't have any. Have you seen the way I'm dressed?" More laughter and applause. "But, if you're offering some of yours, I'll gladly take it and share with all of them." He holds his finger up again. "No, what these ladies want, what they *need,* is some tasteful hooting and hollering."

The veterans of the crowd begin to whistle and hoot. "That's what I'm talking about," Jonathan goads. "But I think you can do better than that. This is a celebration of the human form. These ladies are about to come out here and shake what they've got for your entertainment. The least you can do is give them what they came for. Let me hear it again. This time, let 'em really hear you back there. Tasteful hooting and hollering." The crowd responds.

Then, the side curtain is pulled back. Out steps a tall, dark-haired, olive-skinned beauty wearing not much more than her stockings and high heels. The crowd goes wild. She crosses the stage and plants herself beside Jonathan with a shy curtsy. "Ladies and gentlemen," he calls, "Miss Sara Cha-Cha." The crowd erupts again. Mike can't help but join in with his best whistle. She and Jonathan, who Mike has decided may be the greatest hype man ever, go through a "how to be a good audience" bit. It's hilarious, sexy, and smart.

The drinks are going down easy. Mike decides he was all wrong about this whole burlesque thing. He was right about the crazy hair and tattoos. Probably the daddy issues too. But it may actually be his type of show.

As the crowd cheers yet another performer off the stage, Mike realizes it is already time for intermission. The first half of the night has flown by. Vic grins from ear to ear, calculating every dollar as more drinks are ordered. "I'm going to go check on our performers. Wanna join me?" He grabs a bottle of wine and a stack of cups. "On the house," he says to the bartender, gesturing with the bottle. "You coming?" he asks Mike with a devilish glint in his eye.

Mike considers it, then notices the lines growing longer at the bar, remembering Miss Green Eyes. "Nah, I think they could use some help now. After the show."

"Suit yourself." Vic raises the bottle over his head and makes his way through the people lined up for drinks and the restrooms.

Music plays from the sound booth. Mike opens bottle after bottle until the lines are manageable, and the audience finds their way back to their seats.

"Woo. Don't know where these girls have been all my life, but they are just my type." Vic comes dancing back behind the bar.

"They are all your type, man." Mike laughs.

"True. But these girls are special." He rubs his palms together and grins some more, obviously plotting.

***

"Can you believe that guy?" Bridgette bares her teeth to the mirror, checking for lipstick smudges. She flips her long, fine hair over her shoulder.

"I don't know, Baby. I thought he was cute," Cindy says as she adjusts yet another layer of her elaborate costume. Burgundy velvet and creamy ivory lace hide silky chiffon and glittering corsets. "That pretty golden white boy 'fro does something for me."

"Oh, he's handsome for sure. But didn't he seem kinda sleazy?" Bridgette straightens her dress and gathers her hula hoops.

"They're all sleazy, girl." Cindy gives a knowing lift to her eyebrow in Bridgette's direction. With a shrewd pucker of her lips, she turns to Calvin, "Right, Malcolm?"

"Not me."

"Says the man in a gold lame thong and fishnet stockings," Bridgette says with a laugh.

"Ladies and gentlemen, Baby La Loop," Jonathan announces from the other side of the curtain. The audience is howling before

Bridgette's music starts. She waits for her cue and spins her way
through the curtain, greeted by even louder applause.

"Killer crowd," Jonathan exclaims as he enters backstage.
There's a resounding agreement as the group peeks through the
curtain to watch Baby twirl her way into the hearts of yet another
group of adoring fans.

"She's so damn cute it's indecent." Bunny shakes her head as she
turns to the mirror. "I don't know why I'm nervous. Can't remember
the last time I was." She laughs at herself and starts fluffing her
curls.

"Stop touching it." Cindy slaps her hand.

"Gah. I'm jus—" Thunderous applause cuts her off. Bridgette
comes running back, nearly naked and out of breath.

"That was amazing." She drops her weight onto an empty chair
and sighs. "You look beautiful, Bunny." The little sister Amanda
never had, Bridgette always knew when Amanda could use some
encouraging words.

"Thanks, Baby. I just gotta shake the nerves." She listens for her
cue.

"Coming up next, we got a special treat for you folks."

"What's he doing?" Amanda narrows her eyes.

"We've got one of your own here tonight. This lovely lady is
pleased to be performing here in her hometown. It's been a long time
since she's been back, but here she is. Give a warm welcome to
Bunny Demure." More applause, hoots and hollers so loud, she can
feel it in her chest.

"I'm going to kill him," she says through her stage smile.
Bridgette and the rest of the group smile back.

The music starts. Heat from the stage lights warms her skin. She
can't see the audience, but their applause is the sweetest embrace.
The familiar bass line pulls at her hips. As she saunters across the
stage, she makes love with her eyes to every person in the room.
Peeling off one smooth satin glove with the beat, then, one finger at
a time, the other. The crowd gives her what she came for. She drops
her gown strap off one shoulder and slides it back into place. Batting
her lashes, she plays with them all. Her hands find the zipper of her
gown. She pulls it slowly, seductively. The crowd erupts with
applause and whistles as the dress falls to the floor. She steps out in

stockings, heels, and a hand-beaded corset that catches the light with every sequin.

Another blast of applause, whistles, and hoots. Now the heels. One silky stocking follows the other. Her toes pointed to the very end. She's been told she has legs for days. No more nerves. She is in her element. Unfastening her corset one hook at a time, she turns away from the audience. Her silhouette against the back wall is something she has seen in dozens of clubs, in dozens of cities. But here, it's different. She feels more naked somehow, more raw.

Smiling over her shoulder, she releases the last catch and drops the corset from her waist. Nothing separates her from the world but a sparkling thong and a set of pasties. She turns back to the audience, giving a shimmy to end the song. Cheers and whistles follow her as she blows a kiss and exits stage right.

"Ladies and gentlemen, Bunny Demure."

Chapter Two

"Damn, I'd like to keep that little hula hoop girl on the dashboard of my truck. You know like those little hula girls?" Mike says, leaning toward Vic. The drinks are going to his head. He's taken to talking over the MC in between dancers.

Vic laughs and motions for another round.

"I'm glad you came and dragged me out tonight. Glad I didn't miss this."

"Drink up, buddy." The bartender hands them both a shot of something. Mike knows he'll regret drinking it.

"What the hell. Bottoms up," he says, the shot glass to his lips. "What the…" he lowers the glass and steps away from the bar. "You gotta be kidding me."

"What's up, man?" Vic stands up straight and follows Mike's gaze.

"I thought you'd like her. She seems like you're—" Mike raises his hand, speechless for the moment.

Twelve years. It'd been twelve years since he last saw her. Twelve years since she placed his ring back in his hand and said *sorry* with tears in her eyes. Twelve years since she left him and never looked back. And those years had been kind to her. Back in the day, she'd been all legs and bones. Now she was curves and hips, shimmering in the stage lights like a dream.

Mike rubs his neck. *It can't be.* He steps closer, shaking the buzz from his head. That face, though. It's her. He would know that face anywhere: those eyes, those lips, that smile. How many nights had he dreamt about that face?

His shock fades as cheers and whistles remind him of what's about to happen. He has to fight every muscle in his body not to charge the stage and throw her over his shoulder kicking and screaming. "Bunny Demure, my ass," he says under his breath. Teeth grinding, his fists clenched.

Vic steps behind him. "What the fuck, man? What's going on?"

Mike glowers. "I gotta go." Then he mumbles, "The last shot was poison," and heads for the door.

The heat hits Mike as he pushes outside. Nothing could've prepared him for that. He blows all the air out of his chest, shoves his hands into his pockets, and with his head down heads toward his apartment.

Where has she been? This is what she's done with herself? This is what she left me for? "God dammit." *I'd come so close to forgetting. Should've stayed home.* He shakes his head and walks on. His mind wanders back. Not to that day twelve years ago, but to the years before it.

To the day he met her, eleven years old. Her legs were bruised, knees scabbed over. She was sitting in the sun on the edge of the park, shredding blades of grass, twirling clovers in her fingers. She brought each blossom to her lips and brushed them with a delicate kiss. Tears and dirt streaked her face. Her dark brown eyes looked up at him as he stepped near.

"Hi." She smiled a weak smile and turned back to her flowers and grass.

"What's wrong?" he asked. He wanted to help her, to save her from whatever was making her cry. His hero's heart, as his mom always called it, had kicked into high gear. Not knowing what to do, he dropped his ball and glove to the ground and sat beside her. He didn't say anything. He didn't offer an embrace, but he sat with her. She leaned onto his shoulder and cried. She cried until there were no tears left. Then they sat in silence. Life in the park continued around them. Birds sang, little kids squealed on the playground, and Mike's friends gave up waiting for him. They played ball in the distance.

"Thank you," she said with a tiny voice and another weak smile. Then, she stood up and ran away, setting a precedent for their entire history. He learned later that night that her mom had died recently and she had been moved there by her grieving father to live with an aging aunt. Her name was Amanda Lane. And his life was never the same again.

The sound of traffic brings him to the present. He crosses the road toward his building but passes it. Instead, he pushes on to the river. It's still early and he knows he won't sleep. Memories he's suppressed for years are surfacing. As he looks across the dark water of the Mississippi, he recalls another evening on the river.

Sixteen years old, he'd just gotten his license. They had taken his dad's truck to "fish." He chuckles at the thought. Fishing was code for lying on a blanket in the sand, making out until all their parts ached for more. But not that night. It was midsummer. A night much like the one he was standing in now. He had pulled away from her embrace, expecting the inevitable "no" to come, but it didn't. What he saw in her dark, sparkling eyes was fire. Fire and "yes."

He remembered her long tan legs stretched out in the sand. She bit at her bottom lip, unsure of what to do next. He crushed her to him, taking in every detail. The salty smell of her sun-kissed skin, the sweet sensation of her whole body yielding to him, shifting to fit his completely. What followed was awkward at best but still unforgettable.

He laughs to the sky.

"Unbelievable."

***

"Thank you for coming." Amanda's face hurts from smiling. She and the rest of the group are shaking hands and taking pictures with audience members as they make their way out the door. Everyone is grinning and laughing. "This is why we do it, right?" She leans into Calvin.

He wraps his arm casually around her waist. "Yep. I love making people happy."

"It was a great show. Love this crowd. Such good energy." She smiles more as more people pass by. Calvin is pulled away by a group of middle-aged women. They *have* to get a picture with him.

As the crowd thins out, Amanda turns to the bar behind her.

"Buy you a drink?" That sly, handsome club owner slides up beside her. "What's your poison?"

He's got a face you can't say no to. "I'll have a gin and tonic," Amanda says to the bartender.

"Vic Thornton." He extends a well-manicured hand. Amanda takes it in hers; it's surprisingly soft.

"Aman— I mean. Bunny Demure," she lowers her voice to a flirty whisper and gives her most dazzling smile. Slipping her hand from his, she picks up her drink. "But really, it's Amanda." She reverts to her casual voice and laughs at herself. "Cin is always riding me about using my stage name at shows."

"You guys put on a great show tonight. Impressive." His voice is pure sex. "You're from around here then?"

Amanda scoffs. "Not quite. Jonathan is an idiot."

"Where are you from then?" he asks. *Why does he care?* She couldn't possibly know him. She would remember that face.

"Oh, over the river. A little town. I'm sure you've never been there." She waves her hand in the air in dismissal, changing the subject. "So, I thought you had a partner in crime?" She smiles. "If he's half as charming as you, we might be in some serious trouble here tonight." She lifts one eyebrow and holds his gaze.

"You may have been, if he could hold his liquor, that is." They're locked in a staring match.

"Drinks still on the house?" Cindy wraps her arms around Amanda's waist, peeking over her shoulder. Amanda looks away. Vic looks at Cindy with predatory eyes. *Good luck, buddy*, Amanda thinks. *Cindy may be small. But she's a tornado of a woman.*

"For you ladies? Of course." He's turned his attention to Cindy now. "Are you the one I settle up with?" he asks.

"Mmhmm." Cindy turns up the dial. She releases Amanda from her embrace and slinks between them. Amanda takes her drink and turns to mingle with a group of new-found fans. She looks back to Cindy and Vic's exchange. He's leaned in and dazzling. *Hmm. She may have met her match.*

***

Mike hesitates. Inside that club is possibly the most dangerous woman he's ever met. She's held his heart for nearly two decades. Try as he had to let go, he never could. There hadn't been a single woman in all the years that could make him feel the way she did. These days, she wasn't much more than a box full of trinkets and a couple of old snapshots. Who was he kidding? He still thought of her regularly. Anytime someone introduced him to a woman, saying "she's perfect for you," he'd take her out, have a good time, maybe even take her out a few times. But it never worked. He always compared them to her. And she was just on the other side of this door.

He had wondered so many times what she was doing, where she was. Never had this crossed his mind. *Burlesque? Really? It isn't quite stripping, but I thought she had had more respect for herself.*

All of his questions could be answered if he has the nerve to open the door and ask. She'd always worn her heart on her sleeve. No reason to think she wouldn't share her story with him tonight.

But then, how many years had separated them? For all he knows she's married and her husband is sitting in the club waiting to take her home. The damp heat urges him forward, forcing him to open the door. A couple of patrons push their way through, lighting cigarettes and chuckling together about something they'd seen.

"Here goes nothing."

The chill of the a/c hits him, cooling his sweat-dampened shirt. Johnny Tuesday steps down from the sound booth on his way out for a smoke. Six and a half feet tall and tipsy from the drinks he's been generously supplied by the bar staff, he grins at Mike.

"Kick-ass show tonight. We should book these guys again."

"Maybe, John." Mike's response is short. He's on a mission and not looking for small talk.

He scans the room, looking for Amanda. She's standing at the bar, laughing and flirting with Vic. Mike's heart beats heavy in his chest. He's frozen for the moment, not sure how to approach her.

What do you say to the only woman you ever loved, and who disappeared from your life for over a decade and now she's right in your own backyard? Does she know? Only one way to find out.

She's wearing a shiny robe with brightly colored flowers, her shoulders straight and proud. They show a confidence she'd never known before, walking toward him, looking back, paying no attention to where she's going. He's intrigued by the woman she's become. *What is she like?* he wonders as her laughter dances over the crowd. It's the same deep belly laugh he had heard so many times before. *At least that hasn't changed.*

She runs right into him. Hairs on his arms and neck stand on end. He can smell her, not the perfume, makeup, or hair products. But her. Her skin. Every ounce of him wants to crush her to his chest and breathe deep that smell. To press his face to the soft creamy flesh where her long neck meets her shoulder. He wants to kiss that exact place, and the face that's turning to look at him.

Shock as recognition registers in her eyes.

"Hello, Amanda."

***

Thump. Her shoulder hits what feels like a wall of a man. "Excuse me," she says as she turns to him with yet another stage smile. But that smile fades as her eyes, wide with shock, meet his.

So blue. Blue as the summer sky with flecks of green and gold. She knows those eyes better than her own. Even after so many years. And here they are, towering above her on the face of a man she would barely recognize as the boy she once knew. His copper beard trimmed close frames his perfect lips while hiding the cleft in his chin. *What is he doing here?* Of all the people in the world, he was the last she thought she'd see. She struggles for words.

He finds them. "Hello, Amanda." His voice is low, like silk in her ears. So familiar, yet so strange. What is the edge she hears? Is it anger? Pain? *So many years. He's so calm. Always in control.*

"What are you… How… I'm…." She can't find her thoughts, let alone the right words for the moment. "Oh my god." Tears well in her eyes. A lump grows in her throat the size of a grapefruit.

The silence hangs between them like the years they've been apart. Amanda fumbles to place her drink on a nearby table, falling deeper into his eyes. She closes her own and turns to look at the floor. He doesn't move. She can feel the heat emanating from his impressive frame. In her mind she sees the heartbroken boy asking *why*, so many years ago. She struggles with the familiar urge to run away. But this moment insists on something more. He must be here with his wife, she thinks. No way would he come to a show like this on his own.

"So, what brings you here?" she asks the floor, voice trembling, betraying any sense of confidence she thought she had recovered.

"I'm with a friend." His voice is cold, penetrating right to her soul. "I could ask you the same thing." She can't bring herself to look up. The design on the carpet is the most fascinating thing in the world. Jonathan appears at her side, his arm around her shoulders like a protective brother.

"What'd you think of the show, Mike?" Amanda looks up, surprised to hear his name out of Jonathan's mouth. Her eyes wide, she looks from him to Mike.

"It was great. Full of surprises," he says, his steely gaze set on Amanda.

"Glad to hear it." Jonathan picks up on the intense energy. Always the spokesman, he offers Amanda a way out of the conversation without insulting a fan. "Malcolm was looking for you backstage, Bunny. It seemed important."

"Okay." Her voice is smaller than she expected it to be. She looks at Mike shyly. Not sure what to say.

"I knew a girl once. Used to call her Hunny Bunny when no one was around." Their eyes meet again, and just like that, she's a sixteen-year-old girl stretched out on a sandy river beach counting stars with her best friend.

"Come on, Hunny Bunny, give me some sugar." His voice was so much lighter then, so happy.

"Ugh. Don't call me that." She'd feign disgust and push him away. He'd come at her, and they'd wrestle. Then they'd kiss, and the frogs would sing in the trees.

A warm, familiar feeling creeps into her cheeks. She hasn't felt it in a long time. The shock of finding the last man she thought she would is fading. It's replaced with excitement. "Malcolm can wait. Tell him I'll see him later."

"You two know each other?" Jonathan asks Amanda. He's made it his job to protect all the women of the troupe while on the road.

"You could say that." She looks directly in Mike's eyes. "We're old friends."

A smile touches the corners of Mike's lips. His face softens. She's not sure where the night might take her, but, this is an opportunity she can't ignore. "So, where's your friend?"

Mike nods toward the bar. "You've already met." Amanda follows his nod to see Vic, still laying it on thick for Cindy.

"Are you kidding?" She looks back at him. "Small world."

"Yeah," he agrees.

"Wait a minute." Amanda looks back and forth from Mike to Vic. "Are you the mysterious partner?"

"I am. Prefer silent partner, though."

"How did that happen?" Amanda asks, raising one eyebrow.

"I'm more curious about how all this happened," Mike responds, gesturing to Amanda in her robe and makeup. She looks down, suddenly aware of how exposed she is. One pasty-covered breast about to pop out of her loosely tied robe. She catches Mike's glance down and pulls her robe shut, blushing like she hasn't done for years.

"Let me get dressed. Then we can catch up?" Amanda suggests.

"Let's do that." The coldness is gone from his voice. Her heart races as she scampers backstage.

"Looks like Bunny found herself a bear," Calvin teases as she pulls the curtain back.

"Whatever, Calvin," Amanda responds. "He's an old friend. I can't believe he's here." She drops her robe. "And he owns the place."

"Wait. What?" Calvin cocks his head to the right. "I thought that pretty boy Cin is out there toying with was the owner."

"Yeah, they're partners. Not sure what the story is, but I'll find out." She's pulling on an old pair of jeans and her black A La Mode t-shirt. Running her fingers through her hair, she picks out her curls and looks in the mirror. "How do I look?"

"You look fine, Bunny," Jessica answers. "Where are you running off to so quickly anyway?"

Amanda stops fussing with her appearance and looks at Jessica, Calvin, and Lucy. Jessica is standing in a thong, holding a brush in her hand. Calvin stands beside her, his robe open, revealing his tiny boxer briefs and glittered chest. Lucy's sitting down, pulling off her pasties.

Amanda sighs. "I never told you guys, but before I moved to Chicago, I was engaged. That man out there is my ex-fiancé. We were kids, and I never thought I would see him again."

"Say what?" Calvin asks, peeking out through the curtains again. "Why'd you leave that? Yum." Jessica and Lucy crowd around him to peek out too.

"He's cute," Jess agrees.

"Yeah Bunny. Not my type. But go get 'em, tiger." Lucy nudges Amanda with an elbow to the ribs.

"I don't know, guys. I'm a mess. What do I even say to him?" Her heart feels like it might actually burst. The grapefruit in her throat has returned. "Sorry I ran out on you and went adventuring on my own. You're still really cute, though. Wanna fuck for old times' sake?"

"It would probably work." Calvin laughs as he drops the robe from his shoulders.

"I don't know, Calvin. If he's anything like he used to be, it probably wouldn't. Plus…" She trails off. Her hands are shaking. She feels like a teenager again, remembering the night she left him. The events leading up to that night. The ones that followed. "Shit, you guys. I don't even know, really. There's so much between us. I don't know how to tell him. I don't know what to say." She opens her arms to them. They crowd around for a group hug.

"Say what feels right, Bunny. See where it takes you. You don't have to tell him anything you don't want to," Jessica says as she squeezes Amanda tightly and kisses her face.

"All right then." She pulls away. "Wish me luck. And don't wait up." She shakes her whole body like a dog coming out of the water. "I can do this."

She stands before the curtain, pushing the dark memories deep down inside, then pulls it aside and steps onto the stage. Looking out over the nearly empty room, she wonders how Mike came to own this place. *There is so much I don't know about him. So much he doesn't know about me,* she thinks as she watches him.

He has always been tall. But now, he towers over everyone in the room. He's a wall of a man, all shoulders with strong arms crossed over his broad chest. He's half-listening to something Jonathan is saying, while scanning the room. Cindy and Vic are completely engrossed in their psychosexual game. Bridgette is still entertaining a handful of fans, showing them a few simple tricks with her hoop. One guy is drunkenly trying to keep a hoop up on his hips while his friends laugh.

Mike's eyes meet Amanda's from the back of the house. The butterflies in her stomach are trying to escape. *What am I doing? I can't do this.*

She wants to go backstage and hide again. But it's too late for that. He's seen her. He's excusing himself from his conversation with Jonathan and approaching the stage. She swallows hard and takes a deep breath. Meeting her at the stairs to the stage, he offers a hand to help her down.

She takes it, tingles of electricity traveling up her arm.

Chapter Three

Her hand is soft, softer than he expected, and charged with something that he hasn't felt in a long time. She smiles with her still-red lips. She's shaken out her curls. Her hair is much longer than it looked earlier. A pair of loose-fitting jeans hang at her hips. Her t-shirt is short enough to show a glimpse of her pale belly. It's loose too, hanging off one shoulder as she descends the stairs, her hand in his. This is how he remembers her. Nothing fancy, but beauty, plain and simple. What he wouldn't give to see her face without all the makeup, fresh and clean.

"So, where to?" she asks.

"You wanna walk?" He can't think of anything else. He knows he wants her all to himself. He can't bear to share her with her crazy friends. Or his crazy friend for that matter. "We aren't far from the river."

"Let's do that." She pulls her hand from his and slides them both in her pockets. Mike winces inwardly. He wants to hold her hand again, to pull her close and kiss her mouth, but where would that take him?

She walks ahead of him, approaching Jonathan, who's watching the other performers flirt and giggle.

I don't envy him his job, Mike thinks as he catches up with Amanda.

"I'm going out with Mike," she says, pausing to give Jonathan a quick hug. "Don't worry. I'll be safe." She smiles back at Mike and waves to her friend at the bar.

Sweltering heat meets them as they step outside. "Which way?" she asks, her body painfully close to his.

"The river is that way. If we cut through the alley, there is a strip of clubs and bars right on the next block over." He's pointing this way and that as they cross the street. "We could get a drink. There's a quiet place on the corner." He looks down at her. She's looking at her feet.

"Whatever you want." She looks up. "I'm still in shock, honestly. Can't believe we ran into each other tonight."

"I know. I didn't expect to see you on that stage. Definitely not as much of you…" She stops walking. Mike's two paces ahead of her before he realizes it. He turns back to her. "What's up?" She's standing there under a streetlamp, a hint of rage in her eyes. Her arms are crossed defensively over her chest.

"Are you trying to shame me?" She looks like she might turn and walk back the way she came.

"What?" Mike's not sure how to respond. "What?" he says again. "Why would I want to shame you?"

"Good." Her whole demeanor changes. She lets her arms fall to her sides and walks quickly to meet him with a switch of her hips. "I've already been through it with my dad so many times. Seems he only talks to tell me he's ashamed."

"That's too bad," Mike responds. He never met Amanda's dad. As far as he could see Amanda had raised herself. What right does her dad have judging anything she does?

She shrugs. "It's not a big deal. We were never close. You know that." She smiles. "I'm glad we got that out of the way. I can't tell you how many guys there are who can't handle—" She stops mid-sentence. They are walking side by side again. "I mean, not that many, really." She looks away into the glass storefronts, obviously uncomfortable with where she's taken the conversation.

"Amanda, it's been twelve years. I've been no saint." They walk in silence for a while. Their steps are slow. They've got nowhere to be. "Here's the place I was talking about." They stop in front of a bar with a big train mural painted on the outer wall. Looking through the windows, Mike spots a group of people from the audience having a great time. The thought of walking in with "Bunny" at his side isn't appealing. Not because of embarrassment or shame. He doesn't want to share her with adoring fans.

"On second thought, let's keep walking. That group was pretty rowdy at the club."

"I'm down. Not really feeling Bunny right now anyway. I wouldn't do her justice." He's watching her. She's looking through the window, unaware of his gaze. He wants so badly to touch her cheek, to brush her hair out of her face, to move in and wrap her in his arms. "To the river then?" she asks, looking his way again.

He straightens, diverts his eyes. "Sure thing. It's straight ahead." He motions toward the riverfront. They walk on, leaving the bar crowd to its revelry.

"So tell me how it all started," he says.

"Not until you tell me how you got started," she responds.

"Not much to tell. I met Vic in college. He was my roommate freshman year. We were like brothers from day one. Turned out he was from over the river. After graduation we both came home and went to work. A few years ago, the Speakeasy was up for sale for next to nothing. It was in pretty bad shape. We did a lot of the work ourselves."

Amanda is listening intently as they stroll down the street.

"Vic's done all of the booking and promoting since the beginning. He's really turned it into a great venue."

"So what's your part in the business?"

"I lift all the heavy stuff." He laughs. "No, I was a lot more involved in the beginning. But my demands at the shop have increased over the years. I started working there for my uncle Dick over summers when I was home from college. After his divorce he left it all in my hands. He's been nothing more than a signature on the checks for a couple years now. Last I heard from Dad, old Dick's in Florida spending his hard-earned fortune on Viagra and women too young for him." He laughs again.

She laughs too. They are standing, looking over the river. Rather, she's looking over the river. Mike's looking at her. Drinking her in. The silver moonlight plays on her tousled hair. Her hands rest on the cast-iron rail. Her lips wear a dreamy smile. She turns to face him, eyes full of emotion. "It's been too long."

Mike's heart aches in his chest. *You're the one who left*, he thinks. He bites back the sharp words on his tongue and holds her stare. Her eyes dazzle, as they always have. She wants to say sorry. He can see it all over her face. But she doesn't need to.

He breaks what feels like an eternity of awkward silence. "So, that's my boring story. It's your turn."

***

"Goodness, where to start?" Amanda shifts from one foot to the other, drumming her fingers on the rail. *Keep it light. No need to tell him yet. Don't ruin this moment.* "I was living with my cousin in Chicago. She'd gotten me a job at the club she was working in. I'd never tended bar before, but I was cute enough, I guess. I'd been working about a month or so when Cindy and Lucy came in to perform."

She looks up at the moon, nearly full, hanging in the sky. A gentle breeze off the water cools her sticky skin. The air isn't as heavy. She keeps her eyes on the moon. "They were the most amazing thing I'd ever seen."

She smiles. "Cindy's costumes weren't as extravagant back then, but she had all the moves. Lucy was so damn funny and sexy. They all sparkled so much. Not only the sequins and glitter. I mean they had this radiance about them. And they were so nice.

"After the show, they were gathering their things. I, like the silly country girl I am, gushed and asked more questions than I can remember. They answered them all and encouraged me to come to their next show. I became a super fan. I volunteered to sell their t-shirts so I could get into shows for free. We became friends. One night, after a show they told me they were starting their own troupe and they wanted me to join. I was a stage kitten at first. Picking up their clothes, setting their props, but then I got the opportunity to perform."

As Amanda tells her story, she's taken back to that night in the club. It was intermission, she was organizing props for the second half of the show. Cindy, Lucy, and a few others had stepped out for a smoke break. They came storming in minus one. Daisy La Rue had been causing drama since the beginning. She was always demanding more stage time and recognition. A prima donna like Amanda had never seen. She had been a professional ballerina for some years. This, she believed, made her more qualified than any other in the troupe. "Can you believe this shit," Cindy raged.

"What are we going to do?" Lucy followed close behind. Both were angrier than Amanda had ever seen them.

"She's gonna fucking walk out in the middle of a show just like that." Cindy searched aimlessly through her costume tubs. "Damn it."

"I know. She's right between us in the lineup. We can't fill in for her," Lucy states, a wrinkle of frustration on her brow.

"Plus our contract is for six girls, six routines. Now we only have five." Cindy pauses. "Fucking bitch. I bet she planned this. She wanted to leave us high and dry. Wanted us to look bad."

"You really think so?" Amanda asked. She'd always liked Daisy, despite her super-bitch tendencies, or maybe because of them. "I mean, that's pretty low, even for Daisy." Lucy and Cindy both stopped what they were doing and looked at her. She immediately regretted saying anything at all. She braced herself for the attacks. Instead, smiles stretched across both of their faces as the solution to their current situation became evident.

"You're about the same size as Daisy, aren't you?" Cindy asked, stepping across the room to pluck Daisy's costume off the rack.

"You know her songs pretty well, don't you?" Lucy smiled and winked. They had all seen her dancing off stage and singing along to their routines for months. She couldn't deny it.

"Well, yeah. But I can't dance. Not like Daisy." Amanda had goosebumps from head to toe. She'd been dreaming of this moment since she first saw them on stage. It felt like she had taken a shot of whiskey.

"That's the beauty of burlesque, honey." Lucy moved in and put an arm around her shoulders. "You don't have to dance, so long as you can move."

Cindy brought Daisy's costume to her. "Try it on, at least."

Amanda took the hanger in her shaking hands. "I don't know, guys." Her mouth was unbearably dry, her tongue thick.

"Put it on," Cindy encouraged, rolling her eyes and smiling through her irritation. "You've wanted this opportunity. Well, here it is." Cindy knew how to challenge a person. She knew how to get what she wanted from them too.

"All right. Here goes nothing, I guess." Amanda's heart beat like a caged bird in her chest.

"Yay." Lucy jumped up and down, her huge breasts rippling, nearly spilling out of her tightly laced corset. "What are we going to call you?"

"Good question." Cindy looked Amanda up and down as she struggled with the various snaps and latches.

"She's got a real Marilyn quality about her," Lucy offered.

"Ya, she's definitely got that pinup look down." Cindy moved in to help her with the final adjustments.

"How am I going to get all this off with all those people watching? I can't even get it on." Amanda was more frightened than she had been for a long time.

"Gravity will help," Cindy assured. "And if you get stuck, give 'em that smile and play it up. They love that shit. Fake it 'til you make it, baby."

"Okay, I can do this." Amanda closed her eyes, searching for the confidence she so desperately needed.

"What's your favorite little furry animal?" Lucy asked.

Amanda was looking in a full-length mirror and barely recognized herself. The sparkling corset had her squeezed tight like Scarlett O'Hara, and the garter belt and stockings looked so out of place on her long, skinny legs. "I don't know. I had a boyfriend who used to call me Hunny Bunny," she offered over her shoulder, mesmerized by her reflection.

"Ooh. Bunny. I love it," Lucy cheered, "You look like a Bunny. It suits you."

"It's perfect. That corset suits you too," Cindy said, looking Amanda over with the appreciation of an artist admiring their own work. The color rose in her cheeks in an instant. She looked from her friends to her reflection. "You got to get a handle on your blushing though."

"I disagree," Lucy said. "She's so demure, they'll love it."

"That's it," Cindy exclaimed, looking at her with a satisfied grin. "Bunny Demure."

"And that's how it happened," Amanda says, looking at Mike.

He's been watching her tell her story, his hip leaning against the rail, his arms crossed casually over his chest. He's rolled the sleeves of his lightweight western shirt over his forearms. They're well-defined and the size of her calves.

Her cheeks flush pink as she imagines those arms around her. The top three snaps are undone at his neck, revealing the soft dark hair on his chest. How she wants to run her hands over the expanse of it, to press her cheek there. She remembers the smell of his skin from years before, earthy and warm. He smiles, watching her take him in. From the look on his face she can tell he's reading her mind. She blushes again.

"How'd you do?" he asks, genuinely curious.

"Hmm?" She's forgotten what she was talking about. Her mind somewhere, sharing a mountain of pillows and blankets with him.

"Your first performance?"

"Oh. I was terrible. Got stuck in my corset, ended up running over my song and rushing to my final reveal. The audience was great though. They showed a lot of love. After that, I was hooked. Applause is the most addictive drug. Plus, I had something to prove. I knew I could do better than I had that first night."

"You're pretty good at it now." He smiles. God. How she missed those lips. It had been so long. She'd forgotten how much she loved them. "At least what I saw anyway. I kinda walked out in the middle." He looks away, slightly embarrassed.

"Did you really?" She laughs with a little snort. "Sorry, I mean it's not like you haven't seen it all before."

It's his turn to look out at the water. "I haven't really. Not like that, not like this." He looks at her from the feet up. Then right in her eyes. "You've changed a lot, Amanda."

"So have you." The energy between them is palpable. She takes one step closer. The warmth in the air is nothing compared to the heat radiating from his body. He steps in too. His hand finds hers on the rail. Shocks run from her hand to every point on her body.

Just one touch, and all is lost.

His other hand cups her face, thumb brushing her cheek.

His eyes hold hers with a magnetism she can't deny. She closes hers and leans in. His lips, soft and full, meet hers with gentle longing. She sighs into the kiss, pressing her body against his. His hand trails up her arm, over her shoulder, and down her spine, resting at the small of her back. He pulls her in even closer. A whimper escapes her throat. He answers with a low growl.

Then he pulls away. Suddenly, the hot summer air is cold. She's alone, longing for more.

"I'm sorry," he says.

Amanda stands in a daze. The world shimmers around her. She wants more.

"Don't be."

Chapter Four

Mike looks down at a woman consumed with desire. She's changed so much over the years, she could be a stranger. Had she been, he'd have no hesitation to take her home. But she isn't a stranger. She was the love of his life who had left him.

How many men? How many had held her this way? How many had turned her into this puddle of desire? Those thoughts start a whole new fire in him. Jealousy and rage take over. Holding her at arm's length, his hands on her hips, he purses his lips. "God damnit, Amanda." Her dark eyes are wide. She bites her lower lip. "You really think you can show up like this after everything you did?"

"I don't know what I think, Mike." She steps back, leaving his hands empty. He wants to pull her back and push her away at the same time. He thinks of all the heartache over the years, all the longing. He watches as she turns and walks away slowly, her hand running over the top of the rail. She stops and stands there alone, face turned to the ground. "It's not like I planned this," she says shortly.

"I know. It's just…" He closes the distance she made between them. "This is fucking crazy."

"You're telling me." She's looking anywhere but at him. He reaches for her face, turning her chin to him. Her lips part to speak. She doesn't. No words of protest stand between them. Only pouted lips, flushed cheeks, and eyes that say everything.

"Let me take you home," he says, barely a whisper. She nods in agreement. His place is right across the road.

***

They don't say a word as he leads her across the street, holding her hand. Amanda's heart is in her throat by the time they enter his building. Her head is swimming as he unlocks the door. With the click of the lock and a grin over his shoulder, he pushes the door open. It's dark and cool in his apartment. The streetlights filtering through the blinds offer enough light for her to see where she's walking. He closes and locks the door behind her.

His hands find her waist, creeping up under the loose cotton of her t-shirt. He pulls her against him and nuzzles his face into her hair, breathing deep and pushing it away to reveal her bare shoulder. Bringing his lips to the curve of her neck, he kisses and bites gently. Ecstasy, like warm rain, runs over her. She can feel his cock pressed to her back. Her pussy responds with its own driving pulse. She turns into his chest, feeling his rock-hard excitement prodding at her belly.

With both hands on either side of his face, she drags her fingers through the wiry hair of his beard. His lips find hers, soft and hot. His arms snake around her, crushing her to him. She whimpers as another wave of ecstasy crashes over her with darting tongues and eager mouths. He lifts her into the air, carrying her across the darkened room, down the hall to his bed. Laying her gently on the rumpled sheets, he pushes the blankets aside. She sits up, slipping her t-shirt over her head, tossing it to the floor behind him. He kneels before her on the floor.

With his face in her hands his mouth covers hers then works its way over her chin and down her throat. His rough hands cup her breasts, lifting the weight of them. His thumbs press into her nipples. Her back arches involuntarily. "Ooh," escapes her lips. He presses harder, his mouth covering her chest with delicate kisses. As he finds one nipple, sucking it in on his warm wet tongue, he pinches the other, twisting lightly. She squirms and wriggles, pulling at his shirt. The snaps come undone. He throws it off. Her hands run over the taut, heated skin of his shoulders and back. His hungry mouth moves from one breast to the other. Gently, he pushes her back and slides beside her.

Trailing the knuckles of one hand over her belly, he finds the button of her jeans, and unfastens them with expert fingers. He hooks one under her panties, running it slowly from one side to the other. Her hips rise. With his whole hand over her panties, he cups her mound. She presses down onto it, whimpering as he sucks harder at one nipple. She writhes with each gentle, rhythmic squeeze. "Please." Another whimper.

"Mmmm." His response is more animal than human.

She works her legs out of her jeans. He helps with calloused hands on her silken skin. Rolling to her side, she moves her palm over his chest, relishing the curve of each pectoral. Then, down to his belt. She struggles to unbuckle it with one hand. He moves deftly to help her out, unzipping his pants as well. His cock springs out of his fly. She slides her hand down the smooth, hot length of it.

There's a quiver deep inside of her, accompanied by a knowing that he'll have no trouble reaching it. Her insides throb as she measures his girth. "Oh my fuck." Her words don't matter. Desire is all she can feel.

She tugs at his boxers as he slides her panties down. His hand lingers, squeezing gently at her ass, spreading her cheeks, barely opening her sex. Face to face, body to body, their hands are everywhere. Their lips and tongues dance in the darkness.

She pushes him to his back, straddles him. His swollen tip nudges her clit. She cries out. Her pulsing parts beckon to his. With some effort she slides down on his cock. Her whole body rejoices with tingling joy. She rides, slowly at first. Careful not to take it all in at once. A rolling pleasure from deep in her belly spreads up her spine to the ends of her being.

As it builds so does her pace. His hands run the length of her torso, from her hips to her breasts and back. They clutch at her hips, squeezing them, rocking her with ease. Their breaths are coming faster with sighs and senseless words. He thrusts and she grinds until they are both gripping and panting together in a moment of pure rapture.

Their bodies seem fused as they throb together, floating back to earth. She clings to him, kissing the salt from his chest. His arms engulf her.

***

He is awake. In his arms, he holds a dream. Over the years, he never entertained the thought of her returning to his life. Maybe at first. But after several months had passed, he'd resigned himself to a life without her. She's curled beside him, breath heavy with sleep. The sky grows pale behind the shades. The rising sun casts its rays across the room, landing on her face. She stirs a bit. Then, snuggles deeper into the pillows.

What have you been doing all these years? he wonders as her hair tickles his nose. The smell of sweet flowery hair product reminds him. The night before replays in his mind. First, the shock of seeing her on stage. Then, the flood of memories. Followed by the resolution to make the most of their reunion. And, of course, the reunion itself.

He'd been hard when he woke up. Now, he is throbbing as he thinks of the night before. Of the way her body responded to his. She hadn't yielded. No. She had been in control. The years had changed her. And for the better. He remembers the shy girl who had given herself to him so long ago. Thinking of how awkward it had been, he laughs to himself.

Amanda moves again, beginning to wake. He pushes old memories aside. Focusing, instead, on the woman in his arms.

His hand explores her smooth skin. Starting in the dip of her waist, it follows a silken trail up over her hip, down her thigh to her knee and back. He hovers at her hip again, tracing the subtle jut of her hipbone with one finger. Back down to her waist, up along her rib cage. There, her full breasts are gathered together in a delicious pile. His hand squeezes them both, searching out those beautifully sensitive pearls.

"Mmmm." She rolls to her back, exposing herself fully. "Good morning," she says, eyes still closed. As she stretches, she arches her back. The morning sun dances over her body. His cock aches.

"Good morning." He can't keep his hands off her. Glitter from last night's performance has her sparkling. "Sleep well?"

"Mmhmm. You?" She's turned to him now. The space between them, damn near unbearable. With one hand, he pulls her close, wrapping both arms around her. She's so soft against him. "Oh my." Her dark eyes are open wide, a shameless smile sneaks across her face. "Good morning indeed." She follows with a devilish little laugh as she grips his shaft. She nuzzles her face in his beard and bites at his chin, pulling at him, gently. He slides his hands up and down her back, in step with her pace. "Oh, Mike." His name on her lips has a power over him he didn't expect. His pulse races. She pulls at his earlobe with her lips, whispering, "I want it all."

He moves with a quickness and skill, instantly above her. His fingers search for her wetness, and find it swollen and ready. Her eyes are trained on his, she smiles and bites her lower lip. She lets out a little cry as he enters her completely. Her cheeks flush, her eyes close. He pulls out and does it again, slowly this time. She responds with a satisfied moan. She raises her hips to meet his long, slow thrusts.

"More." That one word and he loses control. Up on his knees, he pulls her by the hips, bringing her down harder and faster upon his thrusts. Her words are unintelligible as she paws at the pillows around her. He lowers himself back over her again, coming down with his full force. She arches and pushes into him. With her teeth in his shoulder, she breathes the word "fuck" over and over, wrapping her long legs around his waist. His heart and pulse race as he loses himself completely.

He collapses in her arms. She holds him close, kissing his face.

***

The pillows smell of him, like sunshine and warm wind. His arm is heavy around her waist. They lie in silence. Amanda can't remember feeling as safe and complete as she does in this moment. But that's all it is. A moment. With one secret, she could ruin it all. Would he hold her so close if he knew the real reason she left? Would he look at her with such kindness and desire if he knew what she'd done? Back home she won't have to think about it. She'll be able to tuck it away in the past where it belongs. She weaves her fingers through his. "It's getting late." Her voice is small. She doesn't want to leave. But she doesn't want to talk either.

"Yeah?" Mike responds, pulling her closer, pressing her to him.

"I'm sure my people are worried about me."

"Let 'em worry." He kisses her ear. "You're a big girl." And squeezes her tight. His affection is more than she can stand. *I don't deserve this.*

"Yes. But they'll want to check out soon. And I left all my stuff at the Speakeasy. I didn't even bring my phone." She sits up, gathering the blanket around her. "Mike." She's searching the room for her clothes. "I have to go."

"I know." His voice is cold. All the playfulness is gone. He stands, pulls on his pants, and crosses the room.

Amanda's chest is tight. Her heart is breaking. But what can she do? It's not like she can walk away from the life she built. The future of Burlesque A La Mode is so bright. Besides, if he knew what she was hiding, he would never forgive her. Best to leave it all in the past for now. Life doesn't have a reset button.

She's watching him as he digs socks out of his drawer. Wearing only his jeans, he's a lovely sight. The lines of the muscles in his back, his bare feet in the carpet. How she would love to stay in this room. So comfortable, it feels like home. He feels like home.

He picks his shirt up off the floor, shakes it out, and slips it on, looking at her. "Well, come on. We gotta get your stuff." Amanda cringes at the sound of ice in his voice. His eyes though. There's a heartbreak in them that she's only seen once before. The day she said good-bye.

"Mike, I..." Her voice falls. They remain still, eyes locked, communicating without words. "I..."

He gives her a forced smile. "Get dressed, Amanda. I'll walk you there." With that, he turns and leaves the room.

Amanda sits, naked and alone, questioning every decision she's made. The life they could have shared. All that could have been. She slips into her jeans and t-shirt, finds her flip-flops and goes to meet Mike in the living room. She hadn't seen much of his home the night before. It's all new to her.

There's a modest-size television on top of a small entertainment center. Across from it, from floor to ceiling, stand two large bookcases loaded with books and random trinkets. The walls are mostly bare, except for one enormous oil painting that she remembered from his parents' house. It was an abstract in earthy reds and yellows. And though it was nothing more than a bunch of splatters and swirls, she'd always seen an autumn woodland scene.

His couch is big and plush. It's the kind of couch to get lost with your lover on, made for snuggles and daydreams. The coffee table is a cluttered mess. There are empty cups and beer cans, a few magazines, a pile of unopened junk mail, various take-out menus, and some loose change.

Mike is on the couch tying his shoes. She wants to sit beside him, to wrap her arms around his neck, to kiss his face and tell him everything that is in her heart. But she doesn't. She stands there, awkward. He looks up as she steps toward the door.

"Ready?" he asks, attempting to sound upbeat.

"I suppose," she says halfheartedly. It's hard to imagine that mere minutes before they were tangled in each other's arms.

He stands and heads to the door. "Mike, wait."

Stopping with his hand on the knob, his head is turned down. "What?" With a flat voice he keeps his eyes on the floor.

"I don't want to leave this way."

He lets his hand fall to his side but doesn't turn around. "Then don't." She can hear his defeat. He turns to her with dampened eyes. "You don't have to, you know."

The raw emotion on his face crumbles her insides. Her throat swells, strangling her response. Pursing her lips, she says, "But I do. There are a lot of people that count on me. I can't pick up and leave them."

Anger flints in his eyes, replacing any sign of heartache. "No. That's treatment you reserve special. Just for me." He pulls the door open with more force than necessary and holds it open, glowering. Amanda swallows hard over the lump in her throat and passes through the doorway.

Mike steps out behind her. *Such a gentleman*, she thinks with some disdain. *Why can't he slam the door behind me and send me packing?* The door closes behind her with a subtle click, and Mike walks on without a word.

His strides are long and hurried, keeping as much distance as possible between her and him as he makes his way down the corridor. She rushes to keep up. "What the fuck, Mike?" She raises her voice. He stops and glares at her. "I don't want this to end. Not like this anyway. Can we please talk about it?" She stops walking, her arms across her chest. Four paces away, he does too.

"What's there to talk about?" His face is calm, though angry fire burns in his eyes. "You have to get back to your life. I understand. Last night was a stop on your tour. You've got things to do. People who need you. I'll be fine." He responds with a tone as sweet as acid.

She flinches, then shrugs it off, determined to make things better. "Chicago isn't that far away," she offers. "I can come back to see you. You can come see me?" Her suggestion is a question. "Anything is better than this." *At least for now.*

"I don't know, Amanda." His countenance softens. Some of his anger dissipates.

"We don't have to know anything, but we can't let it end like this." She holds his gaze and smiles hopefully.

He looks away, out the window at the end of the hall to the street three stories below. "This is too much for this early on a Sunday. Let's get your stuff. You need to get going." He offers a quick half-smile, then heads down the stairs.

Amanda follows, wondering what she'll do when the time comes. Sure that one conversation will end it all.

Chapter Five

Mike pushes open the heavy glass door, holding it for Amanda. The sun is already blazing. He regrets not having his sunglasses. The light, heat, and drinks from the night before are sitting hard on the weight of his current situation. Her smile is restrained as she passes him.

He mirrors hers and follows behind. The silence is agonizing. *But what can I say? "Please don't go"? "Don't leave me again"? Right. Because that worked so well last time.* No, he wouldn't beg. He couldn't beg her to stay. What good would it do? She's on her way back to her real life. How could he compete with the glamorous world she's built? He watches her gentle sway as she walks ahead of him. His eyes squint in the sun. His head and body aches. "Love is a universal migraine," he mumbles under his breath, a line from a poem he picked up in college.

It is love, he thinks. *It always has been.* His pride tells him to stand firm, to walk away. Save himself all the grief. But then, there she is. Something in her walk, in the curve of her hips, tells him to hold fast. The sunlight in her hair gleams. He can't let her go. Her simply being there offers a promise of something more. Something so much more than he's got right now. Picking up the pace, he reaches out to her bare shoulder. His fingers connect with the warm softness. She stops and turns.

Catcalls from across the road stop the words on his tongue. "Ooh, Bunny." A rainbow menagerie of people spill out of the diner in the corner. Whistles and laughter accompany them.

"Looks like someone had a late night." Another voice from the crowd. This one's familiar, though. Vic is standing among them, white undershirt and the same pants from the night before. He has an arm around the waist of one and the shoulder of another woman. From the looks of things, he didn't make it home himself.

"You're one to talk," Mike responds over Amanda's shoulder. He sighs heavily. Her face is alight with hope and guarded expectation. She rolls her eyes at the antics of her "people." *That's what she called them, right?* They are smiling and laughing together, making a scene while getting breakfast. Heads are turning in cars as they pass by.

The tallest one, Calvin if Mike remembers correctly, is absently doing tricks with a hula hoop. His bleach-blond hair and coffee-colored skin are still caked with gold glitter. His booty shorts are the shortest of the whole group.

The redhead is spilling out of a brightly colored halter dress. She's smoking a cigarette with lips painted black. Her husky voice is laughing louder than the others. Vic squeezes the purple-haired one by her waist, whispering something in her ear. The blond hula hooper leans in from his other arm to hear the joke that Mike is sure is at his expense. The three laugh together.

Are they all still drunk? The mysterious dark-haired one leans serenely against the building's wall, saying something to Jonathan. He hadn't changed from the night before either. Except for the hat and coat, that is. He now looks like an actual vagrant. *They're a circus,* Mike thinks, looking from Amanda's casual homegrown beauty to all of their bright colors and personalities. She ran away and joined a circus. How could he compete with them?

"They're crazy," she says with an indulgent smile. Her face all pride and happiness.

"You're telling me." He lets out a short huff. His hand has found its way to her waist, resting comfortably there. It feels so natural to be touching her. So right. "Looks like they are all done."

She looks over her shoulder and back to him. "Yeah. I should probably get moving."

"I'll let you in." He nods toward the Speakeasy across from the diner. The keys jingle as he pulls them from his pocket. His hand slips to the small of her back as they cross the street together. He can't bring himself to break contact. He hadn't known how lonely he was. Up until last night he thought he'd been happy, or content at least. But now, the thought of his bed empty of her was enough to cause a crushing sensation in his chest.

"Come to join us, lover boy?" Vic's smart-ass chuckles resonate as they pass by the group on the corner.

"You're lucky Vic stuck around last night, Bunny," the purple-haired woman chastises as she pulls Amanda in for a hug. "If he hadn't vouched for your guy here, we would have had to tear this town apart looking for you." She looks Mike up and down. "Though I might've run off with him, if you hadn't first." She clicks her tongue in appreciation and raises her eyebrows suggestively. Mike feels objectified for the first time in his life. He understands what Vic had meant when he said they were special.

"Sorry I dipped out. You look like you did all right without me," Amanda teases. "I'm going to grab my stuff." She takes Mike's hand in hers and drags him away from the group, pulling him across the street. Lewd comments and laughter follow them.

"Quite a family you got there," Mike says as he unlocks the door, shaking his head. "That purple-haired one's a real piece."

"Cindy? She's all bark. Really a lot of fluff and glitter on the inside." Amanda flips the bird at the hecklers across the street. "Your friend seems to fit right in."

"He fits in with anyone." A breath of her scent wafts his way as she walks past him through the open door. There's a quickening in his jeans as he realizes they'll be alone again. Locking the door behind him, he catches her by the hand and pulls her back, crushing her to him. She's caught off guard. But her smile says it all.

***

The air inside the Speakeasy is stale. It smells of spilled drinks and sweaty bodies. Amanda crinkles her nose as she scans the dark, empty room. A venue always looks so different after the fans have gone and the stage lights are down, the bones of what it should be. She takes a step into the darkness. Mike pulls her back, crushing her against him. Her heart pounds in her chest. His lips come down on hers, hard, passionate. "I wish you'd stay." His voice is tight with emotion. Her face flushes, heat spreading down her neck and chest, nipples sharp against the cotton of her shirt.

You won't soon enough. "I wish I could." She steals another kiss. "Don't talk." And another. As long as they aren't talking this can last. Her tongue darts quickly over his soft lips; his responds in kind. Electric fingers run shocks up and down her spine. She bites at his lower lip, untangling from his embrace. "One more, for the road?"

she asks coyly, leading him farther into the dark. A ravenous man follows as she walks backwards up the aisle.

Her eyes adjust to the darkness as he catches her at the stage. His large hands clutch her waist, lifting her onto it, pulling her shirt over her head, throwing it behind him. Her hands on his cheeks, she sucks at his kiss. His hands slide under her, squeezing through her jeans, with a rough touch so different from before.

Amanda squirms with excitement, panting. He finds her button and zipper and pulls her jeans off effortlessly. Burying his bristled face in her neck, he works at his zipper and growls, "Look what you do to me." He draws her hand to his throbbing cock. She sighs and strokes from thick base to smooth tip. Its searing heat brushes her naked inner thigh, setting off a small quake inside her.

Gripping her ass again, he pulls her off the stage, bringing her down on his shaft. She's smashed by his forceful thrusts against the brick wall of the stage front. Her legs wrap tightly around him as his fingers dig into her flesh.

She clutches the back of his head, pulling his hair. As he pounds her already battered cunt, she pants and bites at his ear. It's a delicious sort of pain. One that sends tendrils of heat coursing through her. He pulls out, leaving her gasping. But only for a moment. Brusquely, he flips her onto her stomach, her breasts pressed against the cold wood of the stage floor. He pulls her back, giving her every inch of him.

Gasping again as he drives deep in her, she meets each long, hard thrust with bucking hips. His fingers dig in, finding the spot where her hips meet her thighs. She squeals. Exquisite pain forces her to delirium. Each thrust seems to hit deeper and deeper until she's a writhing, pulsing puddle. A guttural cry from Mike's throat and he falls onto her back, hands on her hips, breathing heavy, throbbing inside of her. She lies there, relishing the feeling of their bodies as one, her ribs crushed between his body and a rough wooden plank. Mike gives her hip a squeeze and her shoulder a tender kiss. "I'm sorry," he says, his voice laced with remorse.

"For what?" Amanda says, rising to her knees then standing on the stage. Her legs are wobbly and her vagina may or may not fall out as she crosses the stage to the dressing room. "You gave me something to remember you by," she jokes through the curtain, sitting down next to her suitcase. A nightlight in the corner is surprisingly bright. She looks in the mirror. "Damn." Her reflection is not kind. Completely nude, with raccoon eyes and bedhead. She slouches, poking at her belly rolls. "At least I'm wearing a smile." She laughs and digs some baby wipes out of her makeup bag. Cleaning herself up and running a comb through her hair, she calls through the curtain again. "Could you bring my clothes back?"

Mike appears quickly with her clothes in hand. "You want some light?"

"I'm good. Packed everything up last night. Gotta get dressed and grab my bags, that's all." She takes her jeans and pulls them on. Throwing the same old shirt on too. "I'll get a quick shower at the hotel before we leave. I swear." She looks in the mirror again. "Goodness knows I need it."

Mike lingers behind her, watching in the mirror as she dresses. He's found his clothes, and is wearing his shirt unbuttoned. "Sure you're okay? I lost control out there."

"I'm fine. More than fine actually. Once I get a hot shower, I'll be one hundred ten percent." She smiles and pats his chest before picking her two bags up off the floor.

"I'll take those," he offers, reaching for them.

"Wait."

"What?"

"We won't get to talk once we're out there. I'm sure they're all waiting for us. We won't get a proper good-bye."

"Have we ever?"

She cocks her chin and sighs. "Maybe we should start." She steps to him, wrapping her arms around his waist, pressing her cheek to his bare chest. Breathing in the smell of his skin, she places a kiss right above his heart. He holds her there, running his hands over her back. "I'll call you when I get settled in. Maybe you can come see me?" *Then we can talk.*

"Maybe," he agrees. They hold each other, silent in the poorly lit room.

"I'm so glad this happened." Her voice trembles at the thought of leaving.

"Me too." He presses his lips to the top of her head and squeezes tighter.

"Kiss me." She turns her face to his. He leans in. His lips, so silken, brush hers.

Her phone rings from one of her bags.

"That's our cue, I guess." She wipes at the tears in her eyes, digging her phone out of the side pocket.

"I'm on my way," she answers and disconnects quickly. With sad smiles they exchange numbers and head to the door.

***

It's painfully bright as they step outside. Mike finds himself in a cloud of smoke, perfume, and conversation.

"Hey, Bunny," Calvin drawls. "You lookin' kinda rough." He smiles suggestively, looking Mike up and down. "Fly's down." Mike reaches to adjust his zipped pants. Everyone laughs.

"Eat a dick, Calvin," Amanda snaps.

"Got one in mind?" He gives an exaggerated look around, extending his long neck and torso back and forth.

"We gotta get movin', guys," Cindy chimes in. "Y'all are like wranglin' kittens."

Amanda laughs and shakes her head, reaching to take her bags from Mike. He pulls them away. "I'll carry them for you." She smiles and runs her hand over his bicep.

God damn I wish she were staying, he thinks as the already familiar charge of her touch races to his core. She turns to walk toward the hotel with her fellow "circus folks." Vic falls back to walk with him.

"Good night?" he asks.

"You don't know the half of it," Mike replies, unsure of how much he's willing to share with his friend. "That woman does things to me." He keeps his eyes trained on her round ass as it switches down the sidewalk.

"So what happened anyway? First, you say you aren't doing too hot. Then, you come back and pick up one of the performers. Not an easy feat, I might add. They're a lot more particular than I would have thought."

"You remember Amanda?" Mike asks under his breath.

"Wait. *The* Amanda? The one you were so hung up on in college? The one who made you miss out on all the trim you could've been getting? That Amanda?" Vic mutters.

"In the flesh." Mike purses his lips and nods. "Looks like she got what she was looking for."

"Damn, my friend. Who would have guessed?"

"I couldn't believe it myself. But there she is." As if on cue, she turns, giving him a brilliant smile and some fuck-me eyes. Or maybe, "thanks for fucking me" eyes. His blood rushes in response. He hefts her bags and keeps walking. *Down boy.* She won't be around for a while.

"Kidnapping's still illegal, right? Even if she's an adult?" Mike jokes, trying to make light of the roiling torment in his heart.

"I believe so." Vic chuckles. "Is this a turning point for the long-brooding Mike Nichols? Will you be joining all the happy people of the world now?" he teases.

"Fuck off."

"I'm just sayin' it's good to see you happy."

"I'm happy," he responds.

"For sure. I should say it's good to see you showing interest for a woman. I was beginning to wonder about you." He snickers.

"Whatever, man. I've been plenty interested in plenty of women. Just because I don't have a new one every night doesn't make me uninterested."

"Have you seen some of the women you've turned down?"

"Haven't you seen her?" Mike nods his head in Amanda's direction. For the moment, they watch her in silence. Mike knows Vic can appreciate her beauty. Her pale blonde hair shines in the sun. Her dark eyes sparkle as she laughs. And those lips. Always, those fucking lips. They scream sex, beg for it. Whether they're smiling, trembling, pouting, or shouting, they can drive a man to madness.

They arrive at the hotel. Amanda hangs back as the others say their good-byes over their shoulders and head in. Mike closes the distance between them and sets her bags down. She wraps her hands behind his neck and pulls him to her lips. Her nails drag through his hair as she presses those soft, delicious pillows against his chest. He struggles with the urge to scoop her up and go running down the street with her in his arms like King Kong. Instead, he wraps his arms around her waist and holds her tightly.

"I'll call you," she half whispers, her lips still against his. Another kiss. "As soon as I get home." One more. With her eyes still closed, she holds her forehead against his. "This can work." With that, she turns to go, waving to Vic.

The men stand in the heat of the sun, casting their shadows, as she disappears through the double doors.

***

"Holy shit, Bunny," Bridgette exclaims as Amanda pulls her shirt over her head.

"What?"

"Your back. What the fuck were you doing last night?"

"Looks like she got fucked on some concrete," Cindy says as she steps over to examine Amanda's back.

"Not quite." She blushes, not from embarrassment, but excitement from the memory so fresh she still felt it. "It was a brick wall in the Speakeasy on the stage."

"Damn." Cindy raises an eyebrow. "You went from zero to hoe bag in one night. When's the last time you got laid?"

"Fuck if I know. I haven't been keeping track."

"You sleep in the dining room, girl. We can't help but keep track."

"It's been a while, for sure. But, really. I've been too busy to worry about getting laid. I mean, this…" she says, gesturing to the scratches on her back, "this just happened." She drops her jeans and walks into the bathroom.

"Hurry up. We gotta get on the road."

"I'll be quick." She closes the door behind her. The water runs hot right away. Flipping on the shower, she steps in. Steam envelopes her. She stands, silent, breathing.

Alone.

In a house with six others, alone is a luxury she rarely has. But here in the hotel bathroom, water washing away the sweat of her lover, she feels it like she hasn't for years. Her heart hurts. Tears sting her eyes. The joy she felt mere minutes before in his arms is gone. Now she's so confused. *Everything was going so well. Everything was the way it should be,* she thinks as she absently washes herself with hotel soaps and shampoos. The troupe was getting some recognition. They were finishing their second regional tour. Not a big deal to some. But they were proud. Then, here comes this big, stupid, beautiful man who holds her heart and her past. *What the fuck am I going to do now?*

The hours with Mike flash through her mind like a beautiful, sexy montage. She aches deep inside. Sitting on the bathtub floor, she holds her tender, swollen lips open. The hot water is a shock. But it soothes her still-throbbing parts. She pats herself gently. "It has been too long, for sure," she says, standing up and turning the shower off.

"Come on, Bunny. We gotta move." Cindy pounds on the door. "I got a hot date tonight. Not all of us got fucked into a brick wall last night."

"It was this morning," Amanda responds, wrapping her hair in her towel. "Besides, it's not like you didn't have the chance." She enters the main room. "You and Vic seemed to hit it off pretty well."

Cindy narrows her eyes. "Maybe for him. I was being professional. Honestly, I was more worried about you than anything else last night. You could have at least taken your phone."

"Oh please. It's not like I've ever done this before."

"Exactly. What the fuck were we supposed to think?"

"I told Calvin, Jess, and Lucy what was going on. I figured they'd relay the message."

"They did. And Vic told us what a nice guy Mike is. But they said that about John Wayne Gacy too. And he was dressin' like a clown, rapin' and murderin' folks."

"Oh, come on. That's ridiculous." Amanda rolls her eyes as she digs through her bag for something to wear on the car ride home. "It's not like you haven't disappeared with a stranger for a day or two. Besides, I've known Mike since we were kids. I knew I was safe."

"But we didn't."

Amanda looks up as she pulls her shorts on. It's obvious that Cindy is arguing for argument's sake.

"Well, it was worth it." She smiles a contented smile, reveling in her secret aches and pains. "I don't think I've ever been this thoroughly satisfied." She pauses. "Except all I can think about is when I can get it again."

"Wait a minute. Didn't you say he was your fiancé? Haven't you fucked before?"

"Well yeah. But we were kids then. And…" She sighs. "Let's say he's changed quite a bit since I saw him last."

"So, you're saying he's packin' then?"

"A lady doesn't tell," she jokes. "I'm looking forward to seeing him again."

"I can tell. Now, quit standing there and get your shit together. I'd like to have that freshly fucked glow myself." Most of the group had already headed down to the parking lot ahead of them. Jessica and Cindy were still gathering their things.

"So what happened anyway, Bunny? Why didn't you get married and live happily ever after?" Jessica asked as they walked through the hallway.

"That's a tough one," Amanda answers.

"What do you mean?"

"Short version: I was on a fast track to ruining his life so I left."

"But why? How?"

Amanda considers the question. She knows the answer, but isn't ready to share it. Eyes from every angle in the lobby follow them as they carry their luggage to the door. The Quad Cities likes to claim its hipster credit, but it's a small town whose country roots shine when something out of the ordinary shows up. With giant feather fans, boas, hula hoops, and hoop skirts, Burlesque A La Mode does draw attention. Especially midday on a Sunday. A trail of feathers and sequins surely follow them all the way from their room on the top floor.

"I don't know, Jessica. He was perfect. He was everything a girl could hope for. But he was too good. Too much. I couldn't take the idea of having him and only him forever and always."

"What the fuck, Bunny? That doesn't make any sense. Why would you leave something that was perfect?"

"It makes more sense than you know. At least it did at the time."

"So, now what?"

"That's the million-dollar question, isn't it? I have no idea."

"'Bout time, bitches," Calvin snarks as they approach the already loaded van.

"Sorry, I needed that shower something fierce."

"I bet you did. Dirrrty," he draws out the taunt and laughs at Amanda's expense.

"Whatever." She helps load the rest of the luggage and climbs in the backseat. "You should be thankful. We are about to share a small space. I promise you didn't want to smell me all the way home."

"I don't want to smell you with the shower." Amanda punches his arm as he climbs in beside her.

"You love me."

"Yeah. Now, you got to start talking 'cause I want to hear all about your lost and found-again lover. From the look in your eye, you got a lot to tell."

"Let me wrap my brain around it first, then I'll share some of the good stuff. I'm keeping the best to myself though," she says, pointing to her head. "Keeping it all up here." She looks out the window as the van pulls onto the road. Lucy's in the driver seat. Sublime is playing while the road runs beneath them as they head to the interstate, toward home.

Away from her heart.

Chapter Six

"So, you're going to be a gentleman about this, aren't you?" Vic asks as they walk away from the hotel.

"Whatd'ya mean?"

"I won't be getting the details."

"Oh come on, man. Didn't we grow out of that?" He laughs. "I'll tell you this. Last night changed everything. I've never met a woman like her. Not even when I knew her before. There is a wild sort of thing about her now. Something she didn't have back in the day. It's hard to find words to describe it."

"I hear ya. They've all got it. It's something akin to confidence. But more. Basically, they give zero fucks."

"Yeah. Definitely zero fucks are given."

"So, what happened anyway? This chick pretty much wrecked you. Did she have an explanation?"

"I didn't ask for one."

"What? Why not?"

"Did I need one? We were fucking kids. We could have been making a huge mistake. You know? I wouldn't have gone to college. Wouldn't have started the club. Wouldn't be doing as well as I am now."

"I suppose not."

"She would have lost her goddamn mind too. Whatever she's done with herself, she needed it." He shoves his hands deep in his pockets. Uncomfortable with his current thoughts. "Whatever it's been, I don't think I want to know."

"Can't blame you there." They walk in silence.

"So, how'd your night go?"

"Well, if their behavior says anything about your girl, you can breathe a sigh of relief. They're all business." Vic shrugs. "Couldn't get a single one to crack. Not that I tried that hard. But they were obviously united on the no-booty front."

"No dice then?"

"No dice." He shakes his head.

Mike chuckles. "Shot down."

"In my defense, you have to *try* in order to be shot down. I could read the writing on the wall. Maybe if you wouldn't have run off with one of them…"

"Sorry, man. It had to happen."

"For sure. We stayed at the club and had a few drinks. They kept talking about your girl. Tried calling her until they found her phone backstage. I assured them she was safe. They loosened up a bit. But they were not interested in any extracurricular activities if you know what I mean."

"Too bad." Mike thinks about his extracurricular activities and smiles despite himself.

"We've gotta book 'em again too. Facebook has been buzzing about the show all morning."

"Good deal."

"I thought you'd appreciate that one."

"I do." They arrive in front of the club.

"I got some work to do here," Vic says, nodding to the door.

"Need help?" Mike asks, noncommittal.

"Nah. Books and stuff."

"Cool. I'm gonna head home then. Could use a nap."

"Sure thing. See ya."

"Yep." Vic goes inside. Mike walks home, alone with his thoughts.

Arriving home, he passes through the apartment, a ghost. His head is swimming. His solitude feels more like loneliness. Peace and quiet feels more like empty. There's not a damn thing he can do about it either. He considers a shower. Decides against it, and instead crashes onto his unmade bed.

The smell of sex lingers on his sheets. Glitter dusts the pillow she slept on. Flat on his back, he stares at the ceiling, one arm over his forehead. He slides the other under his pillow. Something soft and lacy meets his fingers. He pulls it out. Tiny black panties. Her tiny black panties. He rolls his fingers over the silky fabric. The urge to smell them is irresistible. Not the crotch, though he's tempted. But the fabric that lay so close to her skin. It must have her scent embedded in it. The urge wins. And there it is, the sweet, delicate essence of her.

The smell takes him back to the night before and beyond. Memories again of so many moments, some innocent and tender, some dirty and wrong, particularly considering the age difference between him now and the girl in his mind. The all-too-familiar ache returns to his chest. He stuffs the silky lace back under the pillow and squeezes back the tears that wet the corners of his eyes. "God damnit." Rolling on his side, he lets the slight hangover lull him to sleep.

***

Amanda dozes next to Calvin. Her body is curled around her knees, her head against the glass. She dreams restlessly of Mike's touch, of his smiling lips, his kiss.

The background chatter of her friends' conversations is a comforting din that lulls her. But she's dying inside, and real sleep eludes her. How could she walk away from him again? It had only been one night and a morning, but everything about it felt so right. She knew that she wanted him in her life. There was no question there. The question was how could she make it work?

Guilt that she's long since dealt with resurfaces. How can she tell him what happened? How can she make him see it was the best choice for both of them? She torments herself. Question after maddening question fills her head to bursting. She wants to scream to the heavens, to pull at her hair and kick at the air, but she settles for a restless shift in her seat and a heavy sigh.

Like a child with a new toy, she can think of nothing but him. She can almost feel his arms around her as she relives her favorite moments that they recently shared. Giving up on trying to sleep, she searches for her phone while contemplating a text message she might send. Maybe he's on Facebook, doubting it. Though her growing obsession is enough for her to look anyway.

"Oh shit," Lucy shouts before Amanda finds her phone. Lucy's completely lost control of the wheel. From the backseat Amanda can see her fighting against it as it rotates back and forth. The van is swerving between the two lanes. A cacophony of scared cries is accompanied by blaring horns as traffic speeds and swerves around them.

"What the fuck?" Amanda shouts. Her heart is pounding in her chest. She covers her eyes. "What the fuck.?" she screams again. Calvin wraps an arm around her and screams as well.

"Fuck, Bunny," he shouts.

With several loud thumps and the grating of wheels on the rumble strips, the van slows to a stop.

"Oh my god. Is everyone all right?" Lucy calls from the driver's seat.

Amanda looks up from Calvin's chest. Bridgette looks up from the other side. He had grabbed them both in the moment, covering both of their heads and faces. "We're all right back here," he responds.

Jonathan and Jessica slide open the doors and spill out onto the grass. Calvin, Bridgette, and Amanda follow. Amanda's hands and legs are shaking. She lowers herself to the ground in the bottom of the ditch.

"I don't know what happened, you guys. Everything was fine. And then the steering wheel had a mind of its own." Lucy lights a cigarette and sits down next to Amanda. Lucy's hands are shaking too as she holds the lit cigarette to her lips. "What was that?" she asks no one in particular. Her gaze meets Amanda's.

"I have no idea." Amanda's body shakes all over as she watches cars and semis fly past. "It was scary as hell though. Glad everyone's okay."

"Me too."

Jonathan and Jessica are looking under the hood. Though neither one knows what they are looking for.

"What the fuck.?" Cindy is sitting in the passenger seat with the door open, her feet on the ground. "That was the scariest goddamn thing in a while. Did you see that muthafucker in the semi? He could have killed us." She holds her lit cigarette in the air. Calvin plucks it out of her hand and leans against the side of the van.

"What do we do now?" he asks, taking a long drag.

"Beats me," Jonathan drawls. "I'm here to book shows and make sure everyone looks pretty. I think this is Amanda's problem. It's her van."

"Shit, guys. You're looking in the wrong place," Amanda says, standing on weak legs. "It's the tire. Look." She walks toward the van. The tire is hanging, nearly perpendicular from the van itself. "What the actual fuck?" She kneels beside it. "How does this even happen? Did you hit something, Lucy? Was there a pothole?"

"Nope. One minute everything's fine, the next the steering wheel went crazy. I don't know what happened."

"Well, shit." Amanda looks out over the flat green terrain. The air is muggy and thick. The sky is overcast and gray. "Have we passed anything recently?"

"Nope. But we aren't far from Galesburg."

"Huh. I really don't want to do this. But Mike is a mechanic."

"Are you serious, Bunny?" Bridgette perks up. "This is a sign. It's the universe pointing the way. You have to call him."

"I don't know about all that," she responds, goosebumps spring up on her arms. "But it does work out in our favor." Amanda is glowing inside at the thought of the whole of existence working to bring her back to Mike's arms. Her independence struggles with the idea of calling him for help. But, as she looks at the broken tire, she knows she has no other choice. Besides, who was she to question the universe?

***

Mike doesn't sleep for long. Emotions are heavy for a man who spent so many years refusing to acknowledge them. The TV is on. Some nature survival show is playing. He's not watching. A book lies open in his hands. But the words mean nothing as he stares blankly at the pages.

Mike checks his phone for the tenth time. She's been on the road for an hour. Of course she hasn't called. He thinks of sending a text, decides against it. She'll call when she gets home. He's sure of it. But then what? Will they spend hours on the phone like when they were kids? Lord knows they've got enough to talk about. What good will the phone call do though? Her voice alone will drive him crazy. He wants to see her, to touch her, to be with her. A phone call will only tease him.

He searches her stage name on Google. Bunny Demure. Images.

There are dozens of tiny pictures for him to scroll through. She's glamorous and beautiful, untouchable even. The woman in the pictures isn't Amanda. The woman in those photos is make-believe: fake hair, fake lashes, eyes and lips painted on. Her beautiful shape is poured and squeezed into so many different costumes. He barely recognizes her. To compare these pictures to the wild woman who shared his bed is almost laughable.

He finds one, though. In the midst of all of the stage pics and promotional shots. She's standing naked in a field. The sun setting behind her. Her face is clean and her hair is blowing in the wind. The light in her eye speaks of her wild nature. It promises of love unrestrained, open, honest, and real. The watermark reads O'Hare Photography.

Mike assumes the O'Hare behind the lens is one of the many lovers she has had over the years. He torments himself with thoughts of their wildly passionate affair. He sees her drinking wine until the sun rises on a blanket somewhere with some sensitive ponytail guy. He imagines her kissing the mysterious photographer and giving him those eyes. The ones from the photo. The ones she gave him earlier that day.

It's too much. He tosses his phone on the couch beside him. Scratching his beard and rubbing his face, he breathes a heavy sigh. No way is this going to work. *It's day one and I'm already driving myself crazy. For all I know, she could be rushing home to someone else. To the guy who took that picture.*

Pacing, he grabs a beer out of the fridge. The first one goes down easy. He pops another open. His phone rings. He rushes like a teenager to answer. It's her.

"Hello?"

"Mike?" Her voice is shaking. She sounds scared. "I'm sorry to call so soon." His throat tightens. He braces himself for whatever might come. "Something happened with my van, and now we're stranded outside of Galesburg. I don't think we can drive it."

Relief. Car trouble is something he can handle. It's also an excuse to see her again.

"What happened?" he asks.

"I'm not really sure. Lucy was driving. She said the steering wheel got a mind of its own, swerved all over the road, then pulled to the right. We're in a ditch now. Looks like the tire is about to snap off." She pauses. "I hate to ask. But is there any way you could come out and look at it? I'm not even sure if anything can be done."

"Are you safe where you are? Away from the road?"

"Yeah."

"Okay. Where?"

"Highway sixty-seven, a little before Galesburg."

"Stay put. I'll be there as soon as I can."

"Thank you, Mike. I wasn't sure what we were going to do. Thank you so much." He could hear her gratitude.

"It's no problem. I wasn't doing much of anything anyway. See you soon. Keep your phone close."

"I will. Thank you again." They disconnect. He hurries to get dressed. From the sound of it she has problems of the major variety. He's going to need a tow truck. Fixing a shitty old van isn't his idea of a great time, but if things work out, he might end up having a really great time.

***

"So, what are we going to do when he gets here?" Cindy asks, her arms across her chest. "Unless he's magic, I don't see this thing moving again."

Amanda raises an eyebrow. "After last night, I'm pretty sure he is." She laughs at her own comment then straightens up. "But, really. He seemed to know what was wrong. I'm pretty sure he'll be prepared."

Someone had pulled some blankets out and spread them on the ground. It's a sticky day. But the breeze from the constant traffic isn't bad. If it weren't so loud, it would be almost pleasant. Calvin and Bridgette play with their hoops in the tall grass. Jessica films them with her phone. Music plays from someone else's. It's a good old-fashioned beach blanket party on the side of the interstate. Amanda and the rest stretch out in the sun.

"Well, spill it then," Cindy demands, rolling onto her stomach.

"What?" Amanda asks.

"I wanna hear the whole dirty story."

"I'm not telling you." She grins.

"Fuck that. You've been holding out on your own Superman since we met you. I want to know where he came from."

"I wouldn't call it holding out."

"Whatever you call it. I want all the details," Cindy says with a flourish of her hands. Lighting another cigarette, she talks through pursed lips. "How do you keep something like being engaged to some hunky country boy from your best friends?"

"He is pretty dreamy, Bunny," Jonathan jokes as he sits beside her. "But, really. I am curious. He's nothing like the guys you go for. I mean, you're more into skinny little artsy types. Like me."

"If you only knew, Jonathan." Amanda throws her hand over her forehead in mock distress. "How my heart pines for you."

"Cut the bullshit, Bunny. I wanna hear the drama. There has to be some."

"There really wasn't. I left. I cried a lot. Then, I left."

"But what about before that? Tell me the whole story."

Amanda sighs. "I guess we have the time." She rolls back onto her back, squinting into the hazy sky. "So my mom died when I was eleven. You all know that. And my dad sent me to live with my aunt. He said he didn't know how to raise a girl. Even as a kid, I knew it for the bullshit it was. I think I looked too much like her. Plus, you can't raise anything when you're drunk all the time."

She shrugs. "Aunt Betty was a bitch. She was old and mean, and less than prepared for a grieving adolescent. I fought with her so much in the beginning. One time, I ran right out of the house. She didn't chase me. I ran to the park down the street and hid in plain sight. My fool ass thought my dad would show up and take me home. He didn't. I cried and cried 'til my eyes went dry. Then, out of nowhere, comes this boy. He came right up and sat next to me. I found more tears, cried some more then ran away." Amanda laughs at herself and shakes her head, wiping at her eyes.

"It was a small town, so he found me pretty easily at Betty's a few days later. We rode bikes and ran around all that summer. By the time school started that fall we were pretty much inseparable. He was my best friend. My only friend, really. We never went steady. We just were. No one even tried to split us up. It was pretty adorable really."

She rolls her eyes and chuckles. "There was this one new kid in junior high. He got a little fresh in the hallway. It was the only fight Mike was in. Poor guy. He was a jerk really. But, I don't know if he deserved the black eye and bloody lip. Hormones raged and we started fooling around. We went to prom together, graduated together. It was a real slice of Americana. You know?"

She sits up and looks at her friends' faces.

"So what happened?" Lucy asks, her nose scrunched up.

"He bought me a ring," she says, giving a sad smile. The truth was hers. The choice she had made so many years ago was hers. She had dealt with it and moved on. Never once did she think it would come back like this. "I took it and said 'yes.' His parents warned us. They gave us so many lectures about real life and marrying young. We wouldn't hear it. Then, one night we were sitting there, planning our future, and I stared at my finger. The tiny diamond sparkling in the light. I remembered my mom's hands. The way her finger grew around her ring. Then, shrank when she got sick. She wore it to her grave. Last I saw, my dad still wore his.

"Then, I looked at my hands. They were young. So soft and childlike. At that moment I realized I had no idea what I was doing. It took me a couple of days, but once I mustered the courage, I gave him the ring back. God it was terrible. I've only felt that kind of emptiness twice in my life." She felt herself drifting as dozens of memories crowded around for attention. She sighs again. "That's the story. Not particularly interesting."

"Ouch," Jonathan says, holding his jaw. "My teeth. That is the sweetest thing I have ever heard."

"Shut up, Jonathan." Amanda shoves him lightly. "It was sweet. And I'm a dick."

"Yeah you are," Cindy exclaims. "But you were right. You did you two a favor."

"I know. But that doesn't make me feel any less shitty about it."

"Lucky for us, he forgave you." Jonathan pauses. "Bitch." They all laugh.

"So, that is sweet and all. But I was looking for a little more. Somethin' juicy or kinky. Tell me about where you got those bruises." Cindy smiles, sitting up on her knees.

"Well shit, Cin. I don't know where to begin. He rocked my world. I've never been fucked like that." She looks at her friend. "He's like this big, beautiful animal…" She trails off, her cheeks get warm. "He's so strong and…" She searches for the word. "Hard." A grin splits her face. They all erupt with laughter. "For real though, guys," she says over them. "It was pretty amazing."

"Speak of the devil," Cindy says, nodding to the road.

"The big, beautiful devil," Jonathan teases.

"This is why I don't talk," Amanda says, standing up.

"Here comes our knight in shining denim," Calvin chimes in from the tall grass.

Amanda watches as Mike backs a tow truck down the shoulder of the road. He stops in front of the van. She sees his boots hit the pavement. Her heart skips a beat as he walks into view. In faded blue jeans, a short-sleeved work shirt, and a baseball cap he's the picture of a good old country boy.

But his eyes promise so much more with a depth and presence that rivals the intellectuals of the world. He smiles when he sees her.

Without hesitation, she runs into his arms.

Chapter Seven

Sweetness and sun-warmed skin, she throws her arms around him. Mike holds her close. Her hair is satin smooth against his cheek. She's fresh and clean. His body responds to hers with quickened pulse and racing blood. He wants to devour her, to gather her in his arms and be the devil in her dreams. But many eyes are watching. And there is work to be done. He presses his lips to her head and pats the small of her back before releasing her.

He scans the area. It's like a damned music festival. Scantily clad ladies hula-hooping and lazing in the sun. "You been hassled at all?" he asks, gesturing to her friends.

"Nope. No one's even stopped to offer help." She shrugs.

"Can you blame them? It kinda looks like you guys want to be here."

"We do bring the party." She smiles and pumps both of her hands in the air. "So, do you know what went wrong?"

"Well, from the sound of it…" He steps toward the van. "And the look, you busted your lower ball joint." He squats beside the tire, assessing the damage.

"What's that mean? Sounds dirty."

"It means this van isn't taking you anywhere today. I can't fix it on the side of the road. I can put it on my truck and take it to the shop, but it might take a couple days." He stands up, turning to face her.

Her face lights up. A smile plays at the corner of her lips. "But that would mean… Well, I'd have to go with it. Right?"

"That's assuming you want to drive it home when it's done." The innuendo, though unintentional, makes him smile.

"It seems like my only option at this point." Her eyes are locked on his. The breeze lifts her hair. She smiles, bright and dazzling. "You know where I could stay for a couple days?"

"I've got a place in mind."

"I bet you do." Her eyes narrow with feigned suspicion.

"What about your crew?" He tips his head toward the group on the blanket.

"I'll go talk to them." She strokes his shoulder as she passes by. Hairs stand up on his neck. He jumps to work. The quicker this is done, the better, and then she's coming home with him.

His back is already damp with sweat as he loads the van onto the truck. The rise and fall of Amanda's voice is obvious among the others. He can't make out what they are saying, but it doesn't matter. In a few hours they'll be in Chicago and, she will be with him.

He works a little faster at the thought. The humidity won't slow him down. Amanda approaches. "I got it taken care of." Mike looks up. She's grinning. "They're taking the train. Got an Uber coming for them now."

"Good," he responds, turning back to securing the van. "They probably want all of their bags, right?"

"Oh shit. Yeah. I guess they do." She turns to them all. "Guys, come get your shit."

They gather at the back of the tow truck. In no time, there is a pile of luggage, neatly stacked on the ground. Mike's impressed by their ability to work so well together with so few words. Maybe there's something to their carny lifestyle after all.

Amanda sits on a suitcase and fans herself. A light sheen of sweat coats her skin. Her tank top clings to her breasts. He busies himself, resisting the overwhelming urge to sink his teeth into her juiciest parts.

"How long till your Uber gets here?" he asks, his voice calm and cool. Though inside it's squeaking like a thirteen-year-old boy's.

"Should be any minute," Amanda says, standing and walking toward him. "Are you close to done?" He looks up into her face. She's as anxious to get moving as he is. He's been making plans since he left his place. He can see in her eyes and the way she moves that she has been plotting too.

***

After a half dozen hugs and kisses, two whispered warnings of unwanted pregnancy, and one very vocal one, Amanda waves good-bye to her burlesque family. She watches silent as they disappear into the distance. Loss fills her heart. The only family she's known for so many years is gone. She knows she'll see them again. But the pang of grief assures her it will never be the same.

How can she go back to living her carefree bohemian life that she's loved so much over the years? How can she go back to sleeping alone in the dining room? Mike steps beside her, placing his hand on her lower back. He's the reason for all the change she feels in her heart. He can also end it in a heartbeat. Once she tells him her secret. The one that only he has a right to. Something about this moment. It's surreal. The blankets are gone. The music and laughter silenced. The tall grass empty, shimmering softly in the breeze. Clouds have rolled in, casting their sepia tone over everything.

"You ready?" he asks, pulling her from her reverie. She turns to him. His brow is knit with concern. His eyes piercing. He can see her sadness.

"As I'll ever be." She smiles with a sigh, not prepared for what has to happen.

"Good. Let's get moving. Looks like we're driving into a storm. I'd like to beat it home."

Home. The word pulls at something inside of her. She's never really known it. Not since she was a little girl. Even with her burlesque family. They are always there. They provide warmth and camaraderie. There is a lovely sense of "being" with them. But they are all sort of lost souls, wandering through existence. The word on Mike's lips is something altogether new. It digs down deep and sings in her cells. She could travel the world, to Neverland and back, and her home would always be here, in his heart.

But, once he knows, will he let her in?

He opens the door to the giant tow truck and offers his hand to help her up. She takes it and climbs in. Her skin tingles where he touches her. Sitting high in the truck, she waits patiently for him to join her. He climbs in beside her, grinning. His eyes sparkle. "I'm sorry your van broke down."

"You don't look sorry," she teases.

"You got me." He turns the key. The truck fires to life. "I honestly couldn't be happier. The last thing I wanted to do today was watch you leave." He checks behind him and eases onto the highway. Once they are safely moving along, he steals a glance her way. His grin has turned into a shy smile.

"Bridgette says my broken van is the universe trying to tell me something." She laughs, watching him watch the road. He snorts a little laugh and smiles.

"Yeah?" He pauses. "What do you think?"

"I don't know. You think the universe cares about us at all? It's a pretty big place."

"I know that as big as it is, we found each other in it again. There's something to that." He steals another quick glance her way. Her heart flutters when their gazes connect.

"True, true. I suppose there's no sense in asking why or how. I'm happy it happened." She watches his profile. He smiles and nods.

"Me too, Amanda." Another look at her, then back to the road. His hand rests on the shifter knob between them. She admires it. Wide and strong with thick fingers stained black from years of work. Golden hairs sprout from the back of his hand, spreading up the taut, ruddy skin of his forearm.

She wants so badly to run her finger along the solid muscle. It twitches as he shifts to a higher gear. She thinks of the intimate moments they've already shared and those to come. He's already impressed her with his skill, surprised her even. She wonders how many women have shared his bed. How many has he loved over the years? She was certain all this time that he had met someone and fallen in love. Certain that a woman who wanted the American dream that he offered had come along and stolen him from the world.

"You know," he says, eyes trained on the road, his voice distant, "it's always been you." It's like he could read her mind.

She cocks her chin, shocked by the connection they share. Or the coincidence. Either way, it's like he picked up on her thoughts. "What do you mean?"

"All these years. All this time. My friends, my family, Vic especially, have been throwing women at me. They've set up blind dates, 'chance meetings,' things like that. I've met some really great ladies, but it never felt right. I never missed them when they were gone. Never wondered what they were up to. I figured I didn't care too much for love." He glances her way, then he exits on the cloverleaf to take them back home.

Amanda sits quiet, unsure how to respond, struggling with the truth. Her silence seems to be his cue to go on.

"I mean, you broke me, Amanda. I'm not going to sit here and pretend like what happened didn't happen." Her cheeks are burning. She shifts in her seat, directing her gaze on the gray storm clouds ahead. "I didn't know which end was up for a while. Didn't know what to do with myself. You were my whole life. And then you were gone."

His words are like knives in her heart. Not in their delivery, but in their truth. Tears sting her eyes. "Don't get me wrong," he says gently. "I understand it all now. Grateful for it even. But we can't ignore the big, ugly elephant in the room." Her eyes shift from the darkening clouds to the dashboard. "Why'd you do it? Why'd you run away and never look back?"

She remains silent, dabbing at the corners of her eyes. Her mouth is dry. The rolling clouds before her perfectly mimic the feelings in her chest. Lightning strikes in the distance. Too far to hear the thunder's roar. She feels like she could burst at any moment, as the clouds promise to do.

She had known the question was coming. It was inevitable, really. Swallowing hard, she tries to wet her lips with a dry tongue. He's given her the perfect opportunity to come clean, to tell him everything. "I don't know, Mike." Her voice cracks. "I was scared. I kept thinking of my mom. Of how she died with so many broken dreams. How all of my dad's dreams died with her." She sighs and wipes at her cheeks. "I'm sorry. I shouldn't be crying." She sniffles. "I just didn't want that for us. I didn't want it for you." She steadies her voice with a deep breath. "God, Mike. You were so good. Too good for me. I loved you. I loved your parents, your whole family. They were all perfect. I couldn't do it. I didn't belong there." It was all true, but she left out the worst part.

His face was stern, cold even. His eyes on the road. "You know that's ridiculous, right?"

"It wasn't then," she responds, her breath shuddering in her chest. "I couldn't see how you could love me as a woman, when you knew me as a child."

"I was a kid too." He raises a brow and looks her way quickly. "We both were."

"Yeah. And look at how much we've changed. We aren't the same people. Not by a long shot."

"A lot of that could be chalked up to circumstance though. We could have grown together."

"Or apart."

"We would have been all right."

"How do you know? It could have been a disaster."

"I suppose it could have. But I don't think so."

"How can you be so sure?" she asks. The silence hangs between them, full of the words they've spoken, and the words they've yet to say.

"Because." He sighs. "I spent years thinking about it. I dreamed about what could have been."

"Me too," she says quietly, remembering the many nights she woke up alone with his smiling face lingering from a dream.

"We would have made it work," he says, still watching the road.

"Yeah," she responds, her voice even smaller, raw with emotions. "Coulda, woulda. It's poison in your veins. Lord knows, I've felt the sting."

"I think we both have." He offers a half smile. They ride in silence, both watching the road and the clouds through the windshield.

"So, what now?" she asks. Nerves frayed by emotion, unable to go on. She doesn't have the courage to say the words. To tell him what really happened and why she left.

***

Mike watches the road, hoping they beat the storm. *It has to hold off for a little bit longer.* Amanda sits beside him. Her eyes are fixed somewhere in the distance. He didn't want to make her cry, didn't want to upset her, but they really couldn't ignore the fact that she broke his heart. That she ran away, leaving him to pick up the pieces. Her right leg is folded under her while the left one lies slightly bent under the dash. Her shorts are so short, most of her thighs are exposed. His hand itches to reach across the console and stroke the soft, smooth skin.

What now? He's searching for the answer himself. "I guess we take it as it comes. Right?" Smiling, he looks her way. She smiles back. Her eyes light up as she blinks away the tears she's been fighting. "We're both adults, right?"

"Yeah." She laughs shortly. "I'm feeling real adult over here." She sniffles again and wipes at her eyes with the bottom of her shirt.

"Shit, Amanda. I expected a lot more tears," he teases.

"The day's not over yet." She laughs at herself and shifts toward him in her seat. Visibly more comfortable. Mike sighs with relief.

On the right, his exit comes up. With a flick of his wrist, he downshifts. The truck slows as he takes the ramp. "Almost there." He smiles, ready to leave the past behind them. She smiles in response. He rolls the window down. The air is noticeably cooler and smells of rain. "We might make it."

His shop is outside of town on an industrial road. It's all but dead on a Sunday evening. Wind tears through the tall grass and shrubs along the shoulder, trees bending to its will. Amanda sits up in her seat, rolling her window down too. The wind rushes through the cab, pulling and whipping at her hair. He watches the rise and fall of her shoulders as she breathes deeply the freshness of the coming rain. He pulls into the lot.

"I'm gonna pull this whole thing in the shop. You can wait in the office if you want," he says, stopping the truck in front of one of the tall doors.

"Okay." They both open their doors and step out. Fat drops of rain hit Mike's face and arms as he hurries to unlock the door. Amanda runs up beside him, rubbing her hands over her bare arms, dancing in place. "Damn. It got cold." The bell on the door rings as they push through. They are met by the familiar smell of fuel, oil, and dust. He flips on the light. Thunder claps overhead. The rain comes down in earnest.

"Made it." He shakes his head, watching as the rain pummels the glass of the door and windows.

"No kidding." They stand together, bodies almost touching.

Mike looks at the rain drops on her skin. She wipes at them. Goosebumps spring up all over her arms. Her nipples poke through the light cotton of her white tank top. He stares and feels that familiar shift in his pants. She steps toward him, placing her hand on his cheek. He looks into her eyes; dark and soulful, they pull him into their depths. She licks her pouted lips. Then, on tiptoes, she presses them against his.

Her pointed nipples are hard against him through two layers of clothes. His cock aches against his jeans. It brushes her belly as she settles onto her feet. He pulls her against him with one hand on her back. The other pinches her nipple through her shirt. "Mmm," she moans against his mouth. He eases her back against the high counter. Then, working his mouth down her neck and over her chest, he gently pushes her back. Her chest is arched up, breasts pointing to the ceiling. He takes one nipple in his mouth, dragging his teeth over the dry cotton. Her hips twist in the air. His hand finds the warm cleft, barely covered by her tiny cutoffs. "Ooh," she whimpers. He pats it gently and nibbles on her tits some more. Her breath is shallow. Her neck and chest flushed with excitement.

"What am I going to do with you?" he asks, his lips against her throat. She smells amazing, fresh and clean. "You." He bites into the skin of her neck. "Are completely at my mercy." He breathes into her ear.

"I am," she responds. Her words slow, drawn out.

"I can do whatever I want." He pats her again, harder. His other hand clutches the hair at the base of her head. She writhes and whimpers. Her eyes snap open as he tugs at her hair. They are glazed with desire.

"You can," she whispers. Mike swells with satisfaction, releasing her hair. He holds her chin in his hand, running his thumb over her lower lip.

"Good girl," he says, his voice low. A look of curiosity flits across her face. He slides his hand under her neck and helps her upright.

Giving her shoulder a gentle squeeze, he steps away. The puzzled look on her face brings a smile to his. "I've got work to do," he says, enjoying her obvious discomfort. "Are you coming? Or you going to stand there and watch the rain?"

She smooths her hair and looks from the window to his face. Shifting from one foot to another, she slides her hands awkwardly in her pockets. He holds the door open and waits. She glances at the countertop and back to him. He can almost hear her thoughts as she passes by.

He reaches for her ass and cups it. She stops. Leaning in to her ear, he speaks in a low even tone. "I've learned a lot over the years." He squeezes hard. "I'm going to teach you all of it." With a quick intake of breath, she stands rigid with excitement. He can feel the

68

heat from her ass. She nods. He gives her a light spank and she walks on.

Mike adjusts himself and follows slowly. *Control yourself.* She doesn't know what hit her. As she looks at him over her shoulder, still confused, he smiles and winks.

***

Mike makes quick work of pulling the truck in and getting the van off the back. Amanda's not sure exactly how he does it. She's in a daze that he put her in. Watching as he easily lifts and moves things she couldn't budge, she tries to imagine what he has in store for her. The rain and wind have the building shuddering. She thinks of the wetness in her shorts and her own shuddering walls. "Oh my," she says under her breath. "What have I gotten myself into?"

Does he have that kind of control over every woman? Or is it only me? It's like some sort of sexy mind control. She laughs at herself, trying to think of another time she felt so docile, so submissive. He could have said crawl: she would have dropped to her knees and followed him anywhere. Even across the grease-stained floor of the garage. And now, except for the occasional nod in her direction, he's all but ignoring her.

He's focused on dismantling her lower ball joints. Meanwhile, she's trying to figure out how he dismantled her psyche in mere moments. *How did he do it??* With the question comes the answer.

He crosses the garage. His long, even strides speak of his confidence. The look in his eyes a promise of what's to come. "There's nothing else I can do without parts." He's wiping his black hands on a pink shop rag.

"Okay. How much is it going to cost?" she asks, realizing that she's already deep in his debt.

"Not sure," he says, nonchalant. "Shouldn't be too much though. I'll call first thing in the morning." He turns away and walks to the oversize sink in the corner. "You ever wash that thing?" he asks over his shoulder, peeling his shirt off. Taking in the view of his brawny chest and arms, she stands in place. He hangs the shirt on a hook on the wall. Starting the water, he lathers soap over his hands and forearms.

"You hungry?" His tone is so casual. How is he not aware of the effect he has on her? Here she is having an existential crisis over his touch while he talks about dirty vans and dinner. Though the mention of food triggers something even more base than the confused lust she's been dealing with. Her stomach grumbles her brain free from the trance he's put her in.

"Now that you mention it, I'm getting hungry." She walks to him, admiring the muscular lines of his back. "Hungry for food and so much more," she says, softly to herself.

"What's that?" he asks over the running water.

"Said I've actually never washed it before."

"It shows." He turns off the water and dries his arms and chest. "Let's get some food. I'm starving." He pulls his shirt over his head. "There's a Thai place over by my apartment. It's pretty good, and fast."

"Sounds good." She's painfully aware of his nearness. His broad, solid chest would be intimidating if she didn't know his kind heart and gentle ways. Though, as her thoughts come back to the scene in the office, she wonders if he is as kindhearted and gentle as she remembers. Heat flashes in her face. *Kind and gentle are overrated.*

"We can get takeout. It'll give us more time for other things." He smiles and pulls her close, planting a quick, playful kiss on her lips before releasing her abruptly. "Let's go."

"Sure thing." She follows him through the door to the office. He's on his phone, ordering takeout. "Wait." She stops. He turns to look her way. "I need my bag," she whispers loudly. He nods in response and talks to someone on the line. She hurries through the door.

The garage is a different place with the lights out. Small windows, high on the walls, let in the light from the cloudy sky. Hoses and machines cast eerie shadows all around. *I can't keep this up. The longer I go without telling him, the worse it will be.*

She makes her way to the van slowly, wondering how to really talk to him. How to tell him her worst secrets without ruining what they have at the moment. She could tell him now. But, surely, he'd tell her to leave. She could stay in a hotel, or she could take a bus home and call the insurance company about her van. They would total it for sure. But they would help her get it out of his shop. "I never should have called him," she says to herself, pulling her backpack onto her back and lifting her suitcase. *Never should have done this. Never should have slept with him. Not without…*

Mike steps up behind her. He takes her bag without a word and carries it to the door. He grins a dangerous grin, setting it down. "It's going to be a while," he says, low and sultry. She sees him moving in.

"Mike, wait." He stops with a puzzled look. "There's more to say." Her throat is closing. "About before. About us." He stands still, eyes steady on hers, lips pursed.

"We were kids, Amanda. Let's leave it at that. Let's put it behind us and enjoy this time that we've been given. I don't want to think of what could have been anymore. That's gone. Nothing we do or say can bring the past back." He pauses and steps toward her. With his head bent down he looks up, considering something. A dark look crosses his face. "You aren't married are you?" he asks honestly without a hint of disdain.

Shocked, she shakes her head, quickly. "Goodness, no. Why would you think that?"

"The way you said that there was more to say. I thought for a moment that maybe you were. But you're not, so, it doesn't matter."

"But—"

"No. I don't want to bring up the past anymore. I have you here. We're together again. And like your friend said, who are we to question the universe?"

"So, we leave it all behind?"

"Yes, for now. Maybe someday in the future we can take out our demons and show them to one another. But for now, let's embrace what we've been given."

She stands, searching his face. Her throat aches with words unspoken, but the coward in her rejoices. *Embrace what we've been given.* "Okay," she says, nodding with a sniffle. "I—"

"Ah-ah, no. It's in the past. What if I say all is forgiven?" His countenance is so sweet and understanding.

She blinks away tears and swallows hard on the pain in her throat.

With a large sigh and a half smile, she agrees, knowing it's not over, but for now she's willing to put it aside for him and for the moments to come. "All right."

He smiles kindly and pulls her into a hug. Then, grinning and mischievous with a sparkle in his eye, he asks, "Should we play a game?" She nods, her cheeks hot.

Bunny, you coward, she thinks as he scoops her into the air and places her lightly on the countertop.

"Unbutton your shorts." His command leaves no room for protest, and pulls her from her thoughts, bringing her to the present. No stranger to undressing for an audience, there is something so wonderfully dirty, raw, and personal about this. She narrows her eyes, cocking her chin with a silent question. *Maybe, you **can** leave it all behind you.* "You said you wanted to play?" he questions softly. His voice is hypnotic. "I said, unbutton your shorts." She does as she's told, shocked by her self-consciousness.

"Now, take them off." She shifts and wiggles out of her shorts. They drop to the floor. Her naked cheeks mash against the cold countertop. "No panties?" he questions. "Aren't you naughty?" he teases, his voice almost tender. She blushes uncontrollably. "Now, take your shirt off. Do it slowly."

She looks him directly in the eye. As slowly as she can, she raises the tank top over her head. She feels her face and ears turn crimson. The air-conditioned chill meets her freshly exposed skin. She shivers. "You're awfully shy, considering..." Amanda opens her mouth to defend her reaction. Mike raises one finger. "I didn't tell you to talk." Her pride urges her to talk all she wants. To bring all of the sass. To tell him what he can do with his game. But his steely gaze promises that it'll be worth it.

"Let me see you." She spreads her arms wide and smiles. "All of you. Put your hands behind your back." She crosses her arms behind her back. Her breasts jut out unnaturally. "I said, all of you." His large, rough hands are warm on her knees as he spreads them as far as they'll go. She trembles at his touch. He steps back to admire her awkward pose. He weighs each breast in his hand, pinching one nipple, then the other. He twists it between his strong fingers until she squeals.

"Shh," he whispers, barely audible.

Amanda's body is on fire. The pain emanating from her nipple, still clenched in his fingers, is exquisite. His whispered command has every tiny hair on her body standing in response. She bites her lip and melts into the sensation. He lets go. She floats on a cloud of relief and agony. The pain is gone. And with it his touch. She pleads with her eyes, silent. Her skin screams for his attention.

He takes her chin in one hand, turning her face toward his. She can feel her cheeks blazing. Never has she felt so real, so exposed. The edge of the counter cuts into her thighs. Her sex, swollen and wet, hovers over the formica. His gaze burns into hers while he's still holding her chin. With his other hand he pets the soft fuzz between her legs, intentionally avoiding her sweet spots. When she thinks she can't take it anymore, he allows one knuckle to brush her throbbing clit. Her body quakes with thunderous joy. Her eyes flutter; she sighs. He holds fast to her chin, taking his second hand away. Her bottom lip quivers. He slows it with his thumb. With their eyes connected, he's in control. She's lost all sense of self.

"You're a good girl," he coos. She's embarrassed and thrilled at the same time. "You have one rule." He pauses, tweaks her nipple again. She winces. "When you're naked, you're mine. You do everything I say. You only speak when asked to, and you don't hesitate. Your body is here for my pleasure. Do you understand?" She nods, unable to look away from the dazzling blue of his eyes. "Tell me you understand," he demands.

"I understand," she squeaks from her dry throat.

A satisfied smile touches his lips. "Good girl." He lifts her off the counter and sets her on the floor. "Now, get dressed." Amanda stands on shaking legs, pulling her shorts up. Mike busies himself with something at his desk.

The power he has over her is overwhelming. Her frazzled brain can't process it. Outside, the storm has subsided to a drizzle. But inside, her body is a torrent of desire. The brush of fabric against her skin is almost more than she can bear.

"Ready?" Mike asks, looking up from his desk. His casual voice holds nothing of the commanding tone he'd been using. She nods. "Good. I'm starving."

He comes around the counter, wiping at a wet spot with a tissue. Amanda blushes. He tosses it in the trash and chuckles, spanking her lightly.

Chapter Eight

Mike watches as Amanda picks at her curry. "Is it all right?" he asks. "I wasn't sure what you'd want. I should've asked."

"It's delicious," she says, smiling over the box. "I'm thinking about…things." She tosses her hair and gives an odd sort of puckered sneer.

He laughs. "What things?" he asks. She's been quiet since they left the shop, watching him with curious eyes.

"Just some…things." She shrugs and picks at her food some more. "It really is great," she says, her mouth full. She's sitting opposite him on the floor, legs crossed under her, shoulders hunched over her food. "I'm…" She looks away from him to the wall. Swallowing, she sighs. "I'm…" She's avoiding eye contact.

"You're what?" he asks, leaning forward from his place on the couch.

"Curious. Confused?" she says, placing her food on the table.

"About what?" he asks, playing dumb. She has to talk. There's a tinge of guilt as he realizes he's enjoying her discomfort a little too much.

"You know what I'm talking about." She lowers her voice like a mother scolding.

"Do I?" he teases.

"You wanna hear me say it. You're going to get some kinda thrill from it, aren't you?" Her tone is mocking, and playful.

He's questioning his decision to "tame" her. Initially, he'd been so pleased to have her back, the thought hadn't crossed his mind. But then she fell into it so naturally. How could he resist? "You do look nice on the floor like that," he pokes, "at my feet."

"Ha." She shoots him a look that might kill a weaker man. But there's something else in her eyes. He can see she's hiding a smile. "Fuck you, buddy." She sneers and stands up, straightening to her full height. "Good luck getting me naked again." She sits on the arm of the couch.

"Is that a challenge, or a request?"

"Neither. You're an asshole."

"Don't say something you might regret later."

"Regret. Humph." She leans against the wall. "I'm glad you're enjoying yourself."

"You know you liked it." She opens her mouth to protest, then stops. "At least, it seemed that way."

"That's not the point here." Her cheeks are pink. "Where'd it come from? That's what I want to know."

"No one's ever asked me that."

"Well?"

"People are boring, Amanda. I mean, I've met some real sweethearts, and some real ball busters, and everything in between. But they all bored the ever-loving shit out of me. It's like they all wanted to talk and talk for hours about nothing. Their mother's friend's something or other. This thing they had to have. Some place they wanted to go. Not interesting places, mind you. Stupid places. Like a restaurant or a club. Somewhere along the line, I stopped listening. I started wondering how far they would let me go."

"Is that what you're doing with me?"

"Not exactly. I mean, it wasn't my intention. But then, you have to admit. It is fun." He looks directly in her eyes. She looks down at her hands and back at him. She smiles with her eyes, all sweetness and light.

"Well, I've never done anything like it before."

"No?" he asks, a bit surprised. She shakes her head. "Good. Then I get to be your first all over again."

"How can you be so sure?"

"Your body has already told me. You're a natural submissive. You just need a master."

"Master? I don't know about all that. You can go master yourself. If you know what I mean."

"Oh, I know what you mean." He stands up to clear the table. "But I also know that you can't wait for more."

"You can't wait for more," she jeers.

"You're right, I can't. And now that we've got your pride involved, it's going to be even more fun."

"I'll show you my pride," she comes back at him.

He laughs at her childish quips. "And so much more." He smiles over the kitchen counter. "Now, why don't you go take a shower?"

"Excuse me?" He chuckles at her irritation. "I'm going to. But not because you told me to, it's because I want to." She stands up and leaves the room.

Mike laughs to himself.

***

"Oh for fuck's sake." Amanda stands in the steamy bathroom. Her shorts and tank lie crumpled on the ground. She wipes the fog from the mirror. Her face is flushed from the hot shower, her eyes bright. "What am I going to do?" she asks her reflection. *He's waiting out there for me. I can't go out in my dirty clothes. But if I go in nothing at all... Well, then I'm asking for it.* "And what's wrong with that?" she asks her reflection again. *Nothing. Nothing at all.*

Leaning in closer to the mirror, she inspects her face. With her sexiest eyes and puckered lips she lowers her voice. "I'm yours." A thrill runs up her spine. Suddenly, she wants nothing more than to walk through the door, or crawl, or whatever it is he tells her to do. Thinking about the way he feels inside of her, over her, her body twitches. "Might as well let him in my brain too," she says as she towel-dries her hair roughly.

She's excited. More excited than she can remember being for sex with anyone. Anyone but him, that is. He was right. People are boring.

Thinking of all the guys she'd been with over the years. They never held her interest for long. She never sought them out. When they came into her life, she'd give them a chance. But it never went far.

It all made sense now. She never left him. Never let him go anyway. He'd always been there, somewhere in her mind. A constant comparison to everyone. A bar set so high, no one could reach it. *But what does that matter now?* He's right there, in the next room. Prowling around, ready to pounce. She's warm and tingly all over. Her tender pink parts are more alive than they've ever been. She wraps the plush oversize towel around her body and looks in the mirror again. *Does this count as naked?*

"Fuck it," she says flatly and drops the towel, opening the door. It's silent in the apartment. All the lights are off, except for the glow from under the bedroom door. She stops in the hall, not sure what to expect. The horrifying image of Mike standing on the other side in a full leather bondage suit complete with gimp mask, whips, and chains flashes in her overactive imagination. *There is no way.* She's hesitant to find out. She walks slowly to the door, listening for rattling of chains. It's silent. *You're ridiculous.*

With a deep breath she knocks softly, unsure of protocol for situations like this. "Come in," he answers lightly through thin walls. Amanda braces herself and opens the door. He's sitting against a pile of pillows on his bed, legs outstretched in jeans and nothing else. *Thank goodness. No mask.* There's a book in his hand. He places it on the nightstand and smiles. "Well, aren't you eager to please?" He stands and approaches her with quick, fluid steps.

"I didn't have m—"

"Did you forget the rules already?" he cuts her off with that smooth, gentle voice. "You should have worn your towel. But you didn't." He looks at her with an almost cruel smile. Leaning in, he breathes in her ear. "You're," one hand runs down her back to her ass, cupping the bottom of one cheek, "all," he squeezes tightly with two fingers and his thumb. She winces but stays quiet. "Mine." He lets go, circling her. The pain of nearly bruised skin radiates into pleasure. She sighs, wanting more.

He steps behind her, close enough that she can feel his heat. "Now, on your knees." She lowers herself, cheeks burning. "Turn around." She does, looking up into his face. Then, to the bulging zipper before her. She reaches for the buckle of his belt, excited to see what's pushing at his jeans. Her mouth waters at the thought, looking forward to reacquainting herself properly. His hand comes down over hers.

"Tsk. Tsk. You weren't told to do that, were you?" His melodic tone is infuriating. *Is he really talking like this? More importantly, am I really responding?*

She looks in his eyes brazenly, hands still on his belt. With his bear paw of a hand still holding hers, she continues working the buckle, challenging him to stop her.

"Are you sure you want to do that?" She smiles and finishes the task. "All right then. Pull it out." She goes for his zipper. He squeezes her hand tightly. "Oh no. I mean the belt."

Her eyes snap up to meet his. Heat flashes in her cheeks again. She narrows her eyes and knits her brow.

"Yes, the belt."

It glides with ease through the loops as she pulls slowly. The whisper of leather against denim speaks to something inside her she never knew was there. The thrill is a surprise.

"Now, turn around and crawl to the bed." She does as she's told. Slowly, as she would on stage, back sloping, ass high. She turns to him with fire in her eyes. Silently asking, *like this?*

He grins and shakes his head, raising his belt up to his chest in both hands. He pulls the loop flat with a crack. Her skin jumps at the sound. She moves quickly, the plush rug soft on her knees. He follows a step behind. "Up on the bed. Face down." His even tone leaves no room for argument.

Obediently, she climbs onto the mattress, looking back as she lowers her face. Mike cracks the belt again. She braces herself. His hand, large and warm, caresses each round cheek. "You weren't so bad really," he says, stroking her all the while. "You only wanted to please me." She relaxes into the bed. Her ass still high. "But…" He stops petting her abruptly. "You did disobey." Warm leather meets soft skin. Once, twice, hard enough to sting.

The pain is exhilarating. Fantastic pleasure rushes from the bottom of her ass to the top of her head. Her breath heaves in her chest. Damp hair sticks to her face and neck. "Ooh," she breathes.

"Shh, shh." He pats her bottom gently with rough hands. Her mind and pulse race. He removes his hand. She waits, suspended in agony, somewhere between his touch and the sharp kiss of his belt. "More. Oh please, more," she whimpers.

The belt falls with a soft thud beside her face. She looks up at him. His eyes sparkle with delight. "You've got a lot to learn." Resting a hand on her hip, he kneels beside the bed. His face is level with hers. "When a punishment is requested, it ceases to be a punishment at all." He pats her gently as he talks. "Then, removing the punishment becomes the punishment." He laughs at himself. "Your first lesson, I suppose, is about desire. Longing for what you want to the point of madness." He stands. "You liked the belt?" She nods, her eyes on his. "Tell me you liked it."

"I liked the belt." Her voice is not her own. He's pulling the words out of her with ease.

Stroking her ass, he asks, "Have you had it before?"

"No."

"Ah-ah." A hard pinch on her soft, fleshy bottom accompanies his words. "I didn't tell you to speak. Remember, no words unless I ask for them." He's petting her as he talks. "Back to desire. The belt is new for you." He picks it up. "You like it. You like the leather on your skin." He runs the belt gently over both cheeks, down and up each long, trembling thigh. "Does it excite you?" She nods. "Good girl." A quick crack against one cheek. "Do you want more?" The supple leather stays still against her. She nods, waiting for more.

He doesn't move. He kneels, holding the belt in place. Its dormancy is driving her mad, as promised. Her skin is alive, clamoring for more. The sting from the first lashes has gone. She sways her hips back and forth against it. He still doesn't move. "You are an eager one." She pleads with her eyes.

He toys with her, tapping the belt gently over her crack. She swells with each tap, backing into it. Her swollen parts are dripping down her inner thighs. He's barely touched her. Yet she can't remember ever being this turned on. His gentle taps lull her into a state of calm acceptance. Though she wants so much more.

As she begins to relax again, he brings it down with another glorious crack. It lands where her thighs meet her ass. She cries out in shock as the belt, like a hot tongue, strikes her swollen labia. Burying her face in the sheets, she raises her hips. She waits for another as they buck uncontrollably. Nothing. After a pause that seems to last a lifetime, he wraps the belt around her waist. He buckles it at the small of her back, bringing the excess to rest over her ass. It dangles like a tail between her legs. With every breath it shifts against her, utter torment.

She turns her head both ways to find him. To say enough's enough. But he's out of her range of sight. She can feel his eyes on her as she shifts uncomfortably, painfully aware of the belt and his presence.

There's a rattle behind her. "Now, put your hands behind your back." She does as she's told, heat rising to her cheeks again. Is it embarrassment, shame, excitement, or all three combined? He straps leather cuffs to her wrists and clasps them to the buckle of the belt. She's helpless. Her face resting on the bed, ears burning at the thought. *Now what?* She pulls at her bonds, testing their strength.

His hand comes down over hers. He squeezes them both. "What to do with you now?" he says softly. His other hand runs over her belly, from one hanging breast to the other. She writhes with his touch, every cell vying for attention. With strong fingers, he pinches and twists one nipple. She shudders, her knees weak. "You like that too?" She nods, eyes closed, breaths slow and heavy, leather tickling her twat.

He pulls at her wrists, lifting her upright with ease. Her damp hair is plastered to her face. She opens her eyes. With one hand he brushes the sticky hair off her neck, away from her forehead, tucking it behind her ear. She leans into his fingertips against her skin.

The last vestiges of her pride fall away when their eyes meet. He holds her face in one hand. She nuzzles it like a cat. Completely under his spell, she'll do anything to feel his hand on her skin. In this moment, she's reborn. Baptized by his touch, by the belt.

He slides his hand over her chin, down to her throat. It lingers there, fingers stroking her tender flesh. One soft squeeze and time stands still. Their eyes are locked together. The thrill of his hand around her throat is indescribable. "You are mine." His statement sounds more like a question. She nods. "Tell me. Tell me you're mine."

He is suddenly more vulnerable than she. Though he could snuff her life out with the clench of his fist. Her words have more power than his hands.

Her heart races. Blood rushes everywhere, hot cheeks, pounding pulse. "I am yours." She's breathless. "I always have been." It's nothing more than a whisper.

Silence, as his hand slips to the back of her neck. He pulls her to him, crushing her lips with his. With his other hand, he presses her to his chest.

"No more games." His words are barely audible. Both of his hands work to free hers. Chains jingle as they fall behind her, along with the belt. Free to roam. Her hands travel his body, over the taut, smooth skin of his shoulders and arms. Then, along his broad solid chest, her fingers spear through his dark hair. Then down, following the trail to his jeans.

One button and a zipper to searing heat of rigid flesh. She pulls her lips from his. Their eyes open, hers wide with delight, his heavy with desire. No more games, he said. She strokes the smoothness of his shaft and squeezes. It pulses in response. She grips tighter. His pants fall to the floor. He kicks them away as his greedy lips find hers again. His hands in her hair, on her neck. She bites at his chin through his thick beard. Kissing her way down, she lowers her face to his cock.

With one hand around the base, she traces her lips with its smoothness. She takes the plump head in her mouth, sucking at it like a ripe fruit. His hands rest on her head as he stands above her. A quick glance up. His head is thrown back in ecstasy. Pulling more in her mouth, she tugs at the base. He grips her hair. The thickness fills her mouth, her tongue can barely work around it.

As it nudges the back of her throat, her insides roll in response. A ripple of sheer joy follows the realization of how much more there is left. With determination she pushes down, past the point where her throat says to stop. All the way down. Until the fine dark hairs tickle her nose. It's like going under water, no air, no breath. He releases her hair with a surprised grunt. Then gathers it back in his grip, pumping slowly in and out. Her hips match his rhythm until she can't take any more.

She sucks at the tip while catching her breath. As she rises to meet him, he looks at her with wild shock in his eyes. Her passion mounts. "Please," she says, stroking him. She kisses his lips, his face, his neck, bristles and heat. "I want you."

Lying back, with knees high, she opens herself to him. He takes her in briefly before lowering to meet her. Throbbing shaft meets dripping folds, pure delight. She's quaking instantly, digging her nails into his shoulders. Wave after wave of bliss washes over her as she rocks with him.

He rises to his knees, dragging her with him, her back still on the bed. With his hands gripping her thighs, his frenzied pumping shakes her. She watches his face. His eyes are closed, his jaw slack. He's lost in the sheer joy of it. Then, his nails dig in. With cock throbbing, he thrusts deeper, bursting inside her.

He's above her again, one hand bracing himself over her head, the other still on her thigh. His eyes open. He grins a shy grin, kisses her tenderly.

***

They lie in comfortable silence. She's nestled in the crook of his shoulder, stroking his chest hair absently. He pets her shoulder and back. "I really liked it," she says out of the blue, rising to her elbow. She looks down at him.

"Me too," he says, giving her a squeeze.

"No, the first part. Your belt, the spankings." She blushes as she says it.

"Did you?" he asks. "I couldn't tell."

"Shut up." The color in her face deepens. She slaps his chest lightly and rolls to face away from him, still wrapped in his arm. Her ass wiggles against his side. He rolls to hold her with both arms.

"Don't be ashamed," he says, kissing her face. "I'm the one who should be embarrassed."

"What do you mean?" she asks, rolling to face him again. "Embarrassed by what?" Her curious innocence is charming.

"I let you get under my skin. That's not supposed to happen. You won."

"I didn't realize it was that kind of game. What do I win?" She smiles, taunting him.

"What do you want?"

"More," she says, running her hand over his chest and stomach. She pulls at his soft sex, bringing it to life with a single touch.

"Careful. You'll end up chained to my bed," he warns.

"Maybe that's what I want." She sits up on her knees and leans over him.

Her pointed breasts brush his chest. She floats around, leaving light satin kisses wherever she may. A nip here. A nuzzle there. She strokes his growing cock.

"Or, maybe, this is all I want," she says, her lips hover over his tip.

She blows, sending a ripple of excitement through him. He tucks his hands behind his head and watches. Her eyes are fixed with delight on his cock. She continues stroking, nudging it with her nose.

She lays kisses along his shaft, up and down, back up. Her face and lips are excruciatingly soft. She takes him in her mouth, wet and hot.

Pouted lips stretch around the girth as she works her hand around the rest. A small laugh escapes him as she inches her way down. Her tongue snakes all over within the sweet, wet confines of her mouth. She slurps hungrily, dipping further. Halfway down, he hits the fleshy wall at the back of her throat. "Ungh. Mmmmm." The sound vibrates throughout him. He twitches. She pushes.

With a subtle pop, he breaks through, all is lost. Slippery and tight, she slides to the base. He grips the pillows beneath his head as his eyes and neck roll in ecstasy. With a sloppy sound she pulls away. The tingle of cool air hits. Then, she's back down, face to base. Warm and moist, up and down. Her hips bounce, undulating in the air. She slips a hand under his balls, cupping and rolling them gently.

Pulling away again, she gulps air like she's drowning. With balls in one hand, shaft in the other, she sucks hungrily at the tip. Pumping her hand up and down. She works it continuously. The luscious sensation builds in him. His muscles tense all over. She slides back down, taking every inch in her mouth and throat. He explodes, with pulsing delight. Pulling away, she suckles, squeezing out every last drop. Her eyes sparkle with self-satisfaction. He chuckles heartily and gathers her to him.

"Looks like you win again."

He kisses her, pulling a blanket over their naked bodies.

Chapter Nine

Amanda wakes to the tickle of whiskers on her face. "Hey, I gotta go." Mike's voice is low and sweet. She rubs sleep from her eyes. He's sitting beside her on the bed, fully dressed.

"Can't you stay?" she asks, running her hand over the stiff fabric of his uniform. It's an unwelcome change from his bare skin. "For a little while?"

"I'm already running late. Besides," he stands, "I've got to get your van fixed." He bends over her to steal another quick kiss. "I brought your bag up. Call me if you need anything."

"Thank you," she says. Though "I love you" sits stubborn on her tongue. It rose so naturally from her heart, but now wasn't the time.

"Make yourself at home."

"I feel like I already have," she jokes, snuggling deeper into his pillows and blankets. He smiles from the door.

"I'm done at four."

"Bye," she says softly. He lingers in the doorway, watching her stretch. Her leg slips out from the covers. The cool air hits her breast as the blanket falls away.

"Ah hell," he says, unbuttoning his shirt as he crosses the room to her. It's on the floor before he reaches the bed.

"Yay," she squeals, throwing the blankets aside. His warm arms engulf her. Their bodies come together in luscious union. Beside her, with his feet still in boots on the floor, one hand holds both of hers above her head as he covers her with bristly kisses. The other runs down her side over her rib cage, her waist, her hip. Back up again to cup one breast.

"If I take off these boots and come back to bed, I'm never going to leave," he says between kisses.

"You don't have to."

"Oh, but I do. There's work to be done."

84

"Well... You can leave your boots on." She pulls her hands free and rolls up onto her hands and knees, wagging her ass near his face. With an appreciative grunt, he leans in, biting it. "Oooh," she squeaks.

He stands behind her, releasing his cock quickly. She turns to him over her shoulder. "Fuck me so hard I can't walk all day."

He pauses for a brief moment, stunned. Then, remembering himself, he gives her hip a tight squeeze. "You asked for it," he says with a fiendish grin.

Sliding in hard and fast, his hips hit her ass. She cries out, feeling him deep in her belly. He grips her hips as he grinds wildly, rocking her forward. Hands splayed before her, she clings to the loose sheets.

He pulls out completely, then fills her again, pumping savagely. Each long, hard thrust shakes her bones. Her entire body is wracked with delight, bordering on pain. One of his hands slips between her thighs. With expert fingers, he plays at her clit. He's grinding again. Amanda wails into the mattress, twitching all over. Sweet release. He clutches her hips again as he finds his. Pulsing and panting, they remain together. He bends forward, brushing her hair away to plant a kiss on her shoulder.

"I really have to go now." He pulls away. She falls to her side, watching him redress.

"I know." She feels him inside her, throbbing when her knees come together. "Glad you stuck around though."

"Me too." He comes back to kiss her lips. It's slow and sensuous, pulling at her heart.

"Hurry back." She sighs into the kiss.

"I will." Smiling brightly, he stands to leave.

She watches as he walks through the door, his shoulders straight and proud. The mountain of pillows meet her as she pulls the blankets up to her chin. Appreciating the understated luxury of the smooth sheets cool against her skin, she slips deeper into the down comforter, soft like a cloud.

He's never been flashy. But over the years, it seems he's developed a taste for the finer things. Sitting up, she looks around. Compared to her little hippie hovel, his room is the Ritz. His dresser and nightstand are of a simple design, but well made and free of scratches. She rolls over and pulls at the drawer. It opens with the smooth ease of quality.

Not like hers, jamming every time. With a hint of shame, she peers in. Instead of condoms and sex toys, as she expected, it's full of trinkets. She fights the urge to paw through it and loses.

Concert tickets, buttons, a pair of cufflinks, belt buckles, two rosaries, tangled from years of neglect. She smiles, remembering the same balled-up relics from his dresser drawer years ago. She snorts at his "Catholic" upbringing.

The randomness continues through safety pins, ink pens, a Zippo lighter. There's a passport, expired. He's much younger in the picture. The passport is old enough to contain stamps from Mexico, Greenland, Canada, all over Europe. Then a stack of snapshots. Mike and his family on vacation, somewhere tropical. It's relatively recent. His parents look great. His brothers grew up as strong and handsome as him, almost. There are wives and children she's never met. Another one, he's in a tux with his brothers. Must be a wedding. Though he's a groomsman, he eclipses the groom with his undeniable sexuality.

Next, twelve-year-old Mike with his dog and first gun. He's dressed for hunting. She remembers that boy. They had so much fun running through the woods together. She'd been the only girl with all the boys. As the years went by, more and more of the boys found other interests.

Eventually, it was only the two of them wandering among the trees. She smiles at memories of simpler times. Flipping to the next picture, it's Mike and Vic in cap and gown. She wonders what they majored in and thinks of all the girls there must have been. The next one is a picture of her and Mike dressed for prom in front of his parents' house. They're so young and awkward. Like children playing dress-up.

She turns the stack over. Each one has his mom's perfect handwriting with names and dates. It makes sense. Of course his mom gave him all the pictures. Where else would such a perfect collection of memories come from? There's another picture. A bigger one. It's a little league team. The kids look about eight or nine. She picks it up to find him in the group. A small thunk draws her attention. Lying there in the dull morning light is the ring. She picks it up gingerly. Twirling it in her fingers, she remembers the day she gave it back.

"I don't get it, Amanda." His young voice was strained with emotion. Tears welled in his eyes.

"I'm sorry. I just can't." Her tears fell freely. Her face raw from the many she'd already cried, mustering the strength to say and do what she'd done.

"What do you mean you can't?" His pain turned to anger before her.

"I can't do this. *We* can't do this. What do we know about getting married? What do we know about anything?"

It had been midsummer. They'd stood in the shade on his back porch. Birds sang all over the beautifully kept yard. His family had always been so good. His mom, who had been cutting flowers when they came through the gate, was an angel. She'd given Amanda so much advice over the years, taking the place of her own mother in many ways. Looking around, she noticed his mom had disappeared. For their privacy, surely.

"We know that we love each other. Right? I mean, I know that I love you. I guess I can't be so sure about you," he spat the words, stealing his jaw.

"Mike, don't." Silence as he looked away. She spun the ring on her finger nervously.

"Don't what?" he asks flatly, quickly wiping at his eyes.

"You know I love you."

"Do I? You've got a funny way of showing it." He sneered. "By leaving? Where are you going anyway?"

"I don't know." More silence.

She stood, shifting in place. She wondered how she could fit in his world. Even after all their years together. She knew she didn't belong. She thought of her aunt's tattered old house. Weeds grew around everything. The grass cut sloppily. He had an amazing, supportive family. She had one evil old aunt and a drunken father who had disappeared.

She was full of brokenhearted baggage. He was well rounded and capable of anything. She spun the ring on her finger some more. She couldn't steal him from the world. She knew what she had to do. She knew he would never let her. There was only one way to save him. She had to leave.

"Well, what are you waiting for?" She'd never heard his voice so cold. He had turned completely away from her. The sobs caught in her throat. She struggled to find the right words, any words. "Just go, Amanda." She pulled the ring off quickly, leaving it on the table. Then she ran as fast as she could away from him.

Amanda dabs her eyes with the corner of the top sheet. The tiny ring sits above her knuckle, too small to fit anymore. With an empty laugh, she removes the ring and returns it to its home.

"We weren't ready. I did the right thing," she says, replacing the pictures and closing the drawer. Her heart breaks for the kids in her memory. But the ache in her vagina is a reminder that it may have been the best-worst decision she'd ever made.

***

Mike fixes Amanda's van easily enough then busies himself with some basic tasks the rest of the morning. After lunch he finds himself sitting at his desk, staring at unfinished paperwork. He can't stay focused. Not knowing she's so close. He thinks of her sitting up on the countertop, naked and bashful. Then, of her that morning, wagging her ass, the exact opposite of bashful. Then, he thinks of her working van, her inevitable departure. His old friend heartache returns, and even after so many years away, it's a crushing empty feeling in his chest. "God damnit." He leans back in his chair and spins around, staring at the ceiling.

"Hey, Mike?" The scrawny kid who insists on being called "D" enters from the shop.

'What?" Mike looks at him, annoyed. All his frustrations held in one word.

"Sorry," the kid stammers. "I was wondering what to do with that minivan? Jim needs the bay." Speaking quickly, he avoids eye contact.

"Shit. I thought I moved it," Mike responds, lightening his tone. "I'll get it." He stands and walks through the door, leaving D to follow.

"So what should I do?" D asks from a step behind.

Mike looks around the shop. Everyone is working. A bunch of seasoned old mechanics need little guidance or supervision. But this kid doesn't know what he's doing. He's always asking what to do next, never taking initiative. Most days, Mike can tolerate it. Today, however, he has little patience.

"Find something dirty and clean it. You can start with the floor here." He points to the van.

"I seen that shit in Chicago," D says, pointing to the sticker in the back window. Mike hadn't paid much attention to it before. There's a big cartoon ass in a g-string and garter belt with a melting scoop of ice cream on top. Inside the scoop it reads Burlesque A La Mode. He laughs at the design. "Those bitches are sick," D says.

Mike's jaw twitches. His fists clench. The idea of this punk-ass kid watching her do anything, let alone dance and strip, sparks a possessive fire he hasn't known for a long time.

"There's this one chick that bends all crazy like a circus freak, except it's fucking hot. Not all freaky like the circus shit." Mike tries not to listen as D goes on about the women's various talents. "There's this redhead with the best tits too." Mike grips the door handle. "I heard their after-parties get real crazy."

He opens the door, turning to D. "Clean the damn floor." He slams the door and drives out of the shop. *What does that jackass know anyway? He's a fucking idiot.* Anger spreads with heat to his face. His imagination goes wild. He sees Amanda on a pole in ridiculous shoes for a room full of guys like D, making it rain with sweaty dollar bills. He cringes at the thought.

It doesn't matter that D isn't really their target market. That two nights ago his club was full of middle-age couples and groups of women. It doesn't matter that there wasn't a single full-grown juvenile delinquent in the crowd that night.

Mike sits in the van, torturing himself with more obscene fancies. He wonders about the after-parties. How would D know anything about them? Not to mention Vic's experience with them. It hadn't sounded too crazy to him. But maybe things were different on their home turf. Maybe they had a group of local fans they liked to swing with.

All those thoughts and more feed his frustrations. Images of Amanda and her friends playing in the raunchiest scenes from the internet torment him. Then, he remembers the way she blushed when he told her to show herself to him. The bashful way she responded to his requests. There's no way she could be spending her nights at some Dear Hustler parties. No way she could be entertaining guys like D after hours. The thought was ludicrous.

He looks at the clock. It's almost two. "I've been here long enough," he says to the empty van. As he steps out, he spots Hillbilly Jim's lanky frame lounging on a stack of pallets. He's smoking and making an art out of ignoring work.

Mike approaches him. "Hey, Jim. Some shit came up. You mind locking up tonight and opening tomorrow?"

"Not at all, boss," he says with a nearly toothless smile.

"Thanks, man. Keep D busy too, would ya?"

"Will do."

Mike nods in Jim's direction and heads in to grab his keys. His bike sits in the back corner. It catches his eye as he passes through. It had been there for weeks. Maybe Amanda would like to go for a ride later. He thinks and plucks his keys from his toolbox. Either way, a good ride will help clear his mind.

It's not the prettiest bike in the world, but it's gnarly and fast. The old Japanese engine fires to life with a familiar wail. Hands on the grips, he kicks it into gear and coasts out of the shop.

With wind in his face and pavement rushing by his feet, he's able to let it all go. No rushing to get anywhere. He follows his favorite back roads. The hills and curves set his mind at ease. The temperature drops as cool breeze blows from shady woods. Then, hot air rises off the sunbaked asphalt as the trees fall away.

Family farms pop up among green fields on his left. The river rambles on his right. He breathes deep the lush sweet smells of summer, remembering the present. Nothing that has happened in the past matters. Nothing that shithead D said matters. All Mike has is the moment he's in. In this moment, the love of his life is waiting for him in his home. In this moment, he should be riding home to convince her to make him her future. Surveying the large empty highway, he slows his bike and pulls a u-turn, his heart full as he heads home. The sun is high in the afternoon sky. It warms his back and urges him on.

The ride home is over in a flash. He's off his bike and hurrying to see her again. The potential of their future together eclipsing any regrets or torments of the past. His heart sinks as he walks into an empty darkened apartment. She couldn't possibly still be asleep he thinks passing through the quiet rooms. The bed is made up. She's not there. His heart sinks deeper still. *Did she pack up and leave? No.* Her suitcase sits, tucked beside his dresser. He sighs with relief.

"She must have gone out," he says, leaving the room. Pleased to know she hadn't disappeared again.

He settles on the couch to take his boots off when her rich, hearty laughter bursts from the other side of the patio door. With the blinds drawn he hadn't thought to look there. Peeking through them, he sees her first. She's stretched out on his patio chair. A light blue sundress covers barely enough to be legal. Her long legs take in the sun while the rest of her relaxes in the shade. One strap hangs off her shoulder, revealing the top of one breast. He knows she's naked underneath and can hardly wait to raise that tiny dress over her waist. She stops laughing and eyes him through the blinds with a smile.

"I gotta go," he hears her say through the glass. "Love you too."

He slides the door open. She sets her phone down and stands to meet him with arms outstretched.

Chapter Ten

Mike's adorable face peers through the window. Amanda is pleasantly surprised. She wasn't expecting him for another hour or so. "I gotta go," she says to Cindy.

"Prince Charming home already? Well, shit. I guess I can cover you at work until Thursday, but we need you Friday night for the show. Remember it's the biggest thing we've ever done. Love you."

"Love you too."

Mike opens the door. She can't wait to touch him.

"Who was that?" he asks lightly.

"Cindy, checking on me."

"Do things check out?" he asks, pulling her closer with one hand.

"I think so," she says with a coy smile. His hand sneaks up her dress to tickle her ass. With both hands on the back of his neck, she pulls his lips to hers. With only a few hours between the last time she had him, she can't believe how hungry she is for his kiss. "I went out today." She kisses him again. "And I got a surprise for you."

"Hm, now I'm curious," he says, his hands making themselves at home up her dress. "But I have a surprise for you too." If she overheard their conversation on the street somewhere between another couple, she might be sick, but here, on his patio, overlooking the river, their playful tones and childish banter seem completely ordinary.

"Ooh. What is it?" she demands, searching him for clues.

"It's not on me. I was thinking we could go on an adventure together. There's some place I want to show you."

"Sounds good. Mine can wait." She thinks of her trip earlier that day. It felt strange at the pet store, perusing the leather dog collars. No one knew it was for her. But she did. That made it feel extra naughty. When she had the dog tag made she couldn't help but blush. With a little clink, the metal heart fell from the machine. She smiled at herself when she read the words inscribed.

"Are you sure?" he asks. "It is a bit of a drive. I'd like to get moving soon."

"Yeah. It's fine." She shakes her head. "It's not much," she adds, scrunching her nose. She's embarrassed now, second-guessing the whole thing. Her plan had been to surprise him at the door in nothing but the collar. But since he got home early, it seems plain silly now. "Yours sounds way more exciting."

"Good. Get what you need for overnight. I'm gonna hop in the shower quick. Also, do you have boots and pants?"

"I've got sneakers," she says, curious. "Where are we going?"

"You'll see." He pauses to take her in. "But first, sit back down." He pushes her gently back onto the lounge chair. "This can't wait," he says, kneeling at her feet. "There's just something about you." Taking one of her feet in his hand, he kisses her toes. Then along the curve of her arch. His beard tickles as he works his way slowly up one leg. Cars rush by below. The hem of her dress barely covers her thighs. His fingers slip under it, inching up over her hips.

"What are you doing?" she squeals, pushing her dress down. She'd been watching people walk up and down the street all afternoon. It was still early. People were still out.

"You know what I'm doing," he says into her thighs, kissing them both. Inching her dress back up again. His warm breath and bristly whiskers send thrills to her core, up her spine, and down to her fingertips.

"There are people out here."

"Yeah?" he breathes, getting closer to her cunt. "So?" His blatant disregard for traffic fuels her exhibitionist tendencies.

He's pushing her dress up more, revealing her hips, her smooth, silken mound. He sucks at her thighs until she's squirming. Tingles of pain fade as he spreads her thighs slightly. His wide tongue warms her already heated folds. The pleasure coursing through her is intensified by this morning's pain. She forgets herself and moans to the sky. Quickly, she looks to the street. There are no bystanders.

"Don't be shy," he says, kissing her thigh, sucking at it again.

She squeals and squirms some more. He clutches her hips, pulling her lower in the lounge. With both hands, he spreads her legs wider. His fingers push gently at her outer lips, revealing her most sensitive parts. He tickles her clit with his darting tongue, then rolls over it slowly, sucking at it with pulsing rhythm.

"Fuck, Mike," she whispers. Her hips rock with him.

He reaches for the top of her dress, pulling it down. One of her breasts falls out completely. He squeezes it and toys with her nipple. She glances down at the street, watching the cars pass. Wondering how many have seen them.

With his other hand, he pushes at one knee, opening her even more. Then, with gusto, he laps at every soaking inch of her. Her legs go numb with delight. Knuckles drag delicately up her inner thigh. Silken tremors follow. She sighs and coos with eyes closed, her face to the sun.

One finger glides inside her. She quakes around it. Reason has gone away. A second finger finds its way. They twist expertly as his pillow-soft tongue works its magic. She grips at his shoulders and pants heavily. A crescendo rising. His pace quickens, matching her breath. She grinds down. Coarse knuckles meet succulent flesh over and over. She cries out, pounding and gripping his shoulders with mad pulsing release.

He slows his pace as she floats on a cloud of bliss. With feather-light kisses on her fuzzy mound, he straightens her dress. Her eyes flutter open. His are shining with satisfaction.

He grins and, without another word, disappears into the apartment.

*****

"Are you kidding me?" Amanda exclaims as they walk through the parking lot toward his bike. "I've never been on one," she says with some trepidation.

"For a big city girl, there's a lot of stuff you've never done," Mike teases. "Will you be all right with this backpack?" he asks, handing it to her.

"I don't know. Will I?" She pulls the bag onto her shoulders, stepping up to the bike. "I can handle a backpack. The rest is up to you." She looks it over, making no attempt to hide her fear.

"I've been riding for years."

"With a passenger?" She looks at him with doubt in her eyes.

Mike laughs. "Yes, with passengers. I will say there is such a thing as a bad passenger, though." He climbs on, looking back at her. "Wanna try it out?" She raises a brow and adjusts the strap of the backpack. "Come on. You know I'll keep you safe." She smiles with a bit more confidence and climbs on behind him.

"But will you keep me alive?" she jokes, with a tremor in her voice.

"Hold on tight and move with me. Don't sit up or wiggle. You'll be fine."

"All right." She sighs. "But if I die, I'll haunt you forever." She slides her arms under his, around his chest, her tits smashing against his back.

Wouldn't be anything new, he thinks as the bike wails to life. She jumps at the sound, clinging to him with every acceleration. She relaxes only at stop lights.

"Where are we going?" she asks over his shoulder.

"That's the surprise," he responds before starting off again. Traffic is heavier than he expected. The bridge is backed up. Cars creep along one, two car lengths at a time. About halfway over they find themselves stopped completely. Cars sit, unmoving all around. Their engines running in time with the rumble of his bike. Music floats out of an open window. Redwinged blackbirds and pigeons fly overhead. Amanda relaxes her hold and sits up.

"This isn't so bad," she says over the din. Her hands rest on his waist. He can feel her shift as she looks around. "The river looks so cool up here. You can see a lot more from a motorcycle."

"Yeah. It's a whole different experience. We're gonna go a lot faster soon," he says over his shoulder, coasting forward. "You ready for it?"

"Ready as I'll ever be. How far is it?"

Cars roll by slowly. He moves to keep up. "Not too far. After we get out of town, it's about a half-hour drive."

"That's not so long." She leans into him. Her arms slide back into place around his waist. Her cheek rests against his back. "I could get used to this part," she says, squeezing him.

"Me too," he responds as they finally start moving again off the bridge, through one of the forgotten ends of the Quad Cities.

Weathered old men lounge in yards of weathered old houses. Industrial buildings sit vacant with windows broken out and doors boarded up. Neon signs from dive bars flash at every other corner. He navigates around potholes, over train tracks, and past closed storefronts. Nearing the edge of town, they pass an ice cream shop.

A sprawling old cemetery with rolling hills stands behind it. Amanda's chest rises and falls against his back. She squeezes him tighter. The shop used to be a Tastee Freeze. They'd spent many summer nights in that parking lot, eating ice cream and dreaming about their future.

Mike pulls into the lot on a whim. There's a small line at the order window. He stops and drops the kickstand.

"Is this the surprise?" she asks, sitting back in the seat.

"No, I thought it would be fun. You remember this place?"

"How could I forget? Ice cream and dead people." Amanda hops off the bike with a grand flourish of her hands. "You remember that night we went exploring back there?"

"Yeah. Remember the tombs in the hill? And the mausoleum on top?"

"No, but now I do. This is the creepiest Tastee Freeze ever."

"You hungry?" he asks

"I could eat." She pats her belly. They step up to the line opposite one another. She leans against the metal railing. He leans on the outcropping window. An elderly couple stands in front of them.

"There's no food where we're going," he says, teasing.

"What?" she asks with a confused grimace. "Where are you taking me?"

"You'll see."

"All this mystery has me wondering…" She crosses her arms over her chest. "What are you up to?"

"Don't worry. It'll be fun."

"Tell me where we're going."

"It's better if I show you."

She cocks her head and glares. It's their turn. They order their food, get their drinks, and find their place at a worn old picnic table. "If you're trying to mess with my head, it's working," she says, sipping her soda.

"Wouldn't dream of it."

"Hm." She watches cars pass. "You're lucky I trust you."

"You're going to love it." Their food is ready. He goes to get it.

Walking back with two white paper bags, he watches her watching cars. Somehow, after all the years, he still sees the sweet, broken girl racing against the heat and her melting ice cream. He considers taking her back to their hometown, to disappear down memory lane. They could visit the park where it all began. Then, find all their old favorite places, holding fast to their lost innocence. He even entertains the thought of taking her to see his parents. They'd be happy to see her. There had been no ill will from them when she left. In fact, they had been relieved. His mom would especially love it.

Amanda had always been the daughter she'd never had. But then, he'd have to share her. He wasn't ready for that. Besides, tonight's not about the past. It's about the present. It's about here and now, and her. He sits across from her with the food, sliding her bag over. "I really can't wait for you to see this."

"Me either."

They eat their burgers and fries, laughing and joking about days past. The parking lot fills up and lines grow. "You ready?" he asks as they bag up their trash.

"Let's go." They hurry to the bike. She climbs on without hesitation. Back on the road, he pulls onto the entrance ramp and accelerates quickly. Amanda grips his shirt, with arms wrapped around him as tight as possible. The late afternoon sun dips lower as they head north through tall shadows cast on the tree-lined highway.

***

Amanda holds on for dear life. The road slips away at a dizzying speed. The wind in her face makes it hard to see anything. Tears stream out of her eyes. She squeezes them shut, leaning into Mike's back. Vibrations from the engine rise up through the seat and course through her body. With one eye open, she steals a glance at the road.

If there was a way to crawl into the backpack on her shoulders, she would gladly do it. It's not an option, however. So she clings even tighter to the man in front of her. She feels a pat on her left calf. He's driving with one hand. Her initial reaction is to scream and hold on tighter. Then she realizes how safe she must be. If he's willing to devote one hand to comfort her, they couldn't possibly be in any danger. He isn't showing off. That isn't his style. As his hand returns to the handle grip, she relaxes a bit. Their pace has been set, no more jerking or shifting gears.

With her cheek still against his back, she looks out over fields of corn and soy. Patches of trees dot the landscape. Old barns catch light from the lowering sun. The scent of thousands of red clovers and goldenrod swirl around her with the rushing wind. Her hair whips and billows along with it. A joy she hasn't known for many years rises up inside. And the tears are no longer from the stinging wind but the aching beauty of it all. Their hearts had been calling out to each other for so long. Finally, they are where they should be, mere inches apart. Separated only by the flesh and bone that protect them.

As they fly down the highway, challenging death with every mile, she leaves the world behind. All the nights painting her face, shaping her hair, molding herself into Bunny Demure disappear. The applause she sought for so many years loses its appeal. She's unsure where they are going but can't wait to get there.

From highway to country road, the bike slows. Oversize houses with beautiful lawns and long drives spring up on either side of the road. Large vegetable gardens in full bloom complement the beautiful homes. The houses crowd closer together and shrink as they get closer to a town smaller than their own. They slow to a stop at the only sign.

"How are you holding up?" Mike asks, patting her leg again.

"I'm all right. I had to get used to it."

"Good. 'Cause here comes the fun part."

"The fun part?" she asks, sitting up, adjusting herself in the uncomfortable seat.

"There's gravel coming up. But only for a bit. Then we'll be there."

"Good."

He starts off again, slowly at first. She wraps her arms around him. This time with less fear and more excitement. At the edge of town they pick up speed. The country roads dip and wind past man-made lakes and fields full of straw bales.

Daylilies, bright and orange, bend toward the sun along the shoulder on either side. They slow and turn onto a dirt road, passing cattle and horse farms so close she can see the texture of the animals' fur, the glisten of their eyes. Then they hit gravel. Choking dust and flying rocks force her to bury her face again. It's over quickly enough. They're back on dirt.

Amanda looks up. Trees and tall prairie grass greet her. The sun's golden light is tinged pink as it inches behind the trees, casting its fiery glow on everything. They ease along the curving dirt road, deeper into the trees. The air is cooler along the shady path.

"I'm definitely hearing banjos now, Mike," she says over his shoulder. She feels his laughter against her chest.

"Don't worry. I'm the most dangerous thing here."

"That's what I'm afraid of." They turn again, down a road she wouldn't have found on her own. The trees fan out to an opening. A small cabin glows in the setting sun. Behind it, giant sycamore trees arch out over a glittering river.

He stops the bike, killing the engine. Her ears adjust after the noisy ride. Birds and bugs sing in a myriad of voices. The river chimes in with its own lovely melody. "Oh Mike. It's beautiful," she breathes, climbing down.

"I knew you'd love it," he says, coming up behind her and taking the backpack from her shoulders.

"It's pretty amazing." They walk together toward the riverbank. He drops the bag on the picnic table. They stand in silence. She absorbs it all. The freshness of the air, the blushing radiance of the waning sun everywhere, the dark shadows that complement it all so well, and the trees rustling in the breeze couldn't be more perfect. That is until Mike pulls her close. His lips find hers with the most heart-wrenching tenderness.

"Want to check out the cabin?"

"Yes." They're like children sharing secret treasures.

The screen door bangs behind them as they step onto the screened-in porch. A cracked old lounge chair sits next to a plastic table, holding its weight in empty beer cans. Through the main door, Amanda is met with a flood of nostalgia.

The one-room cabin looks like teenage Mike's bedroom with a kitchen. Old movie posters and clippings from *Weekly World News* share wall space with funny postcards and printed quotes laced with sarcasm and wit. There are street signs and license plates, tin signs with sexy pinups, and a girly calendar opened to May from two years ago.

There's a full-size bed covered with flat pillows and old quilts, a loveseat with an afghan thrown over it, and a small bookshelf in the corner. A small wooden table sits in the kitchen area with one chair.

The fridge and stove are small and dated. There is no television, only on old radio on the counter.

"It's not much," he says, shrugging.

"It's perfect." She smiles, so full of love she could burst. Love for the man in front of her, and the boy she once knew.

"I've never brought anyone out here," he says, almost shy.

"Really? Why not?"

"Well... the banjos for one." He smiles and laughs.

"Yeah, I suppose if you weren't you, I would have been pretty nervous on those last few turns."

"But, really. This is for me. It's where I go to get away. I've never cared to share it before."

"That makes a girl feel awfully special."

"You are special, Amanda." Her heart flutters with glee. His sparkling eyes hold hers.

"So are you." Unspoken words of love and devotion sit stubborn on her tongue. She steps closer to him. He meets her in the middle of the room, his arms pulling her in. He kisses her lightly.

"We need a fire," he says with a quick squeeze before letting her go.

"Ooh, yes," she coos.

The thought of lying by a fire with him under the moon is almost too much. She follows him outside. Firewood is stacked neatly under the porch. He pulls out several large pieces. Amanda sits on the top of the picnic table, her feet on the bench.

The firepit sits between the table and the river. Mike pulls a long-handled axe off the shed wall and kicks a thick log upright. She watches quietly, content with her view. In only a white undershirt, his muscles bunch and stretch with each fluid swing of the axe. The log splits in two under the weight of his swing. The ease with which he works through the wood shows years of perfecting his skill. Not to mention his strength. Lust simmers in her core as she continues to watch. He smiles at her between logs.

"You wanna get some sticks together?" he asks, bringing the axe down again with a crack.

"Sure." Feet crunching around the edge of the woods, she gathers as many sticks as she can. From tiny to as big as her thumb, she remembers what he taught her years ago about how to build a fire.

She pauses to watch him from behind. Every smooth movement is intentional, controlled. With another splitting blow to the wood, images of his belt cracking in his hands come to mind. The phantom sting of it against her ass starts a whole different kind of fire. He's oblivious to the effect such a simple act has on her. To him, he's chopping wood. To her, it's a display of all his raw sexual energy. His strength, his control, his power over the world around him are all on display in this seemingly simple process.

She drops her sticks in a pile by the firepit and wanders in another direction for more. Into the trees, along a worn path, she walks. The sun is all but gone. Though the sky is still light, its colors are fading. The trees no longer cast shadows. They sit peacefully in the muted blue light of dusk. Frogs and cicadas begin their songs in the trees. She finds another handful of sticks and hurries out to the open. Mosquitos have joined the party. She's eager to be free of them.

Mike is kneeling by the fire ring, tiny wisps of smoke rising already. *Is there anything he can't do?* she wonders. "Got any bug spray?" she asks, swatting at the hungry bugs.

"Yeah. I also have some incense sticks in there. If we light a few of them, it usually keeps the bugs away." He's feeding larger sticks to the fire. "They're both in the cabinet above the stove. You wanna grab the blanket off the bed too?"

"Anything else we need from inside?"

"There might be some beer in the fridge, if you're interested."

She heads in, screen door banging behind her. Stripping the quilt from the bed, she bundles it under one arm. Its sweet, salty musk speaks of all the nights Mike slept under it. She grabs the incense, leaving the bug spray behind, not wanting to smell or taste like poison. Then to the fridge.

The front door is plastered with stickers from bands and performance parts as well as a random sprinkling of words from a magnetic poetry set. She laughs at the memory of them writing silly poems for each other on the inside of his locker door. Mike was right about the beer. In fact, it and bottled waters are the only things in the fridge. She takes two cans and heads back out. The fire is already burning bright. Mike relaxes at the picnic table.

Amanda sets the beers behind him and spreads the blanket out next to the blazing fire. "How many should I light?" she asks, opening the package of incense.

"The more, the better," he says, opening a can and taking a hearty swig. She pulls out four and lights them in the fire, then sticks one in the dirt at each corner of the quilt. The perfumed smoke spirals up, sweetening the air.

She settles onto the blanket and stretches. Mike's eyes are on her. She smiles and lies back, watching the birds and bats fly and dip through the darkening sky. Fireflies float up from the grass like glowing green bubbles. Their silent dance is hypnotizing. There are too many to count as they float around, beginning their ascent to the trees. The rhythm of everything around them is one great lover's song. All the creatures are looking for mates. Amanda knows in her bones she has found hers.

Chapter Eleven

She's perfect. The moment is perfect. The sheer joy on her face borders on innocence as she watches the fireflies. "It's crazy seeing you here."

"Hmm?" she responds, her eyes bright with simple pleasure.

"In all my years, and all my daydreaming, I never thought you'd be here with me."

"No?" She knits her brow. "I guess I never imagined it myself." He moves to lie beside her. "All I thought I had was memories."

"We've got plenty of those." He places a hand on her hip, wishing she were wearing less.

"You were right. I do love it here."

"I knew you would."

"There's not a lot of opportunity for camping back home. Plus, I don't know who would do all the work." She laughs and tosses her hair over her shoulder. "I mean, can you see Calvin chopping wood and building a fire?"

"No. No I can't. Maybe your buddy Jonathan. But even then, I think you might be the best woodsman out of them all."

"Everything I learned, I learned from you." She rolls onto her stomach, chin resting on her hands. Mike moves his hand from her hip to the small of her back. She's watching the fireflies again. He's watching her. The fabric of her shirt is hot from the blazing fire. He runs his hand up her back and down again. It finds a new home, resting on her denim covered ass.

The silvery blue light of dusk fades. Orange light dances over her face, casting lovely shadows. "I'm not ready to be thrown out to the wild or anything." She laughs. "But I know my way around a campfire."

"Do you? When was the last time you had to start one?" he asks, one eyebrow raised.

"You don't believe me?"

"It's not that I don't believe you. I'm curious when you had the opportunity."

"Well, it's been a while." She looks at him, then up at the sky, shaking her head and smiling.

"Would you say it's been twelve years or so?" he teases.

"Yeah," she responds, her voice dropping low. Looking away, she falls silent.

Regret sits heavy on Mike's chest. He wishes he could unsay it. "Amanda, I'm sorry. I didn't mean anything. I was only—"

"It's all right. I know. You just reminded me." She looks down at her hands. "Everything I've missed, everything we could have had together." She looks back at him. Her eyes wet and gleaming.

"Don't think about that now. You're here. We're here, together. That's what matters."

"I have to leave soon though. I've got to be back by Friday." His heart breaks over her words. He knew it was coming, knew this wasn't forever.

"I figured as much. You have a show?"

"Yeah. It's a pretty big deal. The biggest venue we've ever been in. A real theater." They share their silence. Night's song surrounds them, ignoring their discomfort. His hand lies heavy on her as he searches for the words that might repair the moment.

"Hey," he says gently. "Don't think about it now. It's only Monday. We're out here, in the middle of nowhere. Time pretty much stops here."

"I suppose you're right." She takes a deep breath. "No need in fussing over the inevitable." Her words are like daggers in his heart again. *The inevitable. Does it have to be inevitable?* He's known she was leaving since she came back into his life. But *inevitable* sounds so permanent. He swallows his pain, smiling for her sake.

"I could keep you here chained to my woodstove. No one would ever find you. Hell, my parents don't even know where this place is." She tilts her head, squinting one eye.

"I'm not sure if I should start running or become a willing captive. Would you at least feed me?" she asks, relieved to be speaking of lighter things.

"Whatever you'd like." He strokes her back. "Shit, I'd even give you a chain long enough to reach outside."

"Outside even? Wow, you really know how to treat a girl."

"I sure do," he says. "Wait a minute. Didn't you have a surprise for me?" She blushes, looking down at her hands.

"It's silly," she says, shaking her head. "I think I left it at your place anyway."

"Damn. I was looking forward to it."

"Don't. It was nothing, really." She smiles and rolls back to her side, facing him. "So, how'd you find this place anyway?"

"I knew a guy who was looking to get rid of it. It's a lease right now. But I hope to own it someday. This cabin and the fifty acres around it."

"What would you do with all of it?" she asks, sitting up.

"I'd move out here for good, build a new place, live off the land. It's not a glamourous life, but it's my dream. I've been working for it for years now."

"It sounds perfect," she says, her eyes fixed in the distance.

"What about you? What have you been working for all these years?"

"I don't know. That's the rub. It's like I've been running since the day I left you. Not toward anything, just away. The closest thing to a goal I've had is finishing the next show. Renting a fraction of a duplex and sleeping in the dining room is hardly an accomplishment." She looks at him then back to the distance. "You've done so much over the years."

"Not really. I've worked and I've saved."

"You own a bar, Mike. I work in one."

"You're performing. That's hardly working in a bar."

"I perform, sometimes. Most of the time, though, I'm tending bar. That's how I support myself. Burlesque doesn't pay dick."

"Really? You'd think...I mean, those costumes don't look cheap."

"They aren't. It takes a month of shows to break even on one."

"Wow. But you love it, right?"

"Yeah. It's exciting. Touring is fun. Applause is addictive. I guess there are festivals. But I've never even thought of applying. I mean, I've been having fun with it." She shrugs, and looks out at the darkness behind him. "I rarely know when I'm scheduled to work next, let alone what I'm doing with my future." She looks back at him with a weak smile. "That's until I saw you." She sighs. "Now, all I can think about is the past and…" She bites her lower lip and looks away.

Mike's up on his elbow, lying on his side. He can see her discomfort. He wants nothing more than to take her in his arms and kiss it all away. Her dark eyes pierce his with a pain he didn't expect. One he recognizes from his own reflection. "How the fuck am I going to leave you?" The tears start before her words are finished.

"You don't have to." He sits up and gathers her into his arms. Sobbing shakes her body against his. "You don't ever have to," he says again, softly as he strokes her hair away from her face. She sits up, looking at him.

"But what about everything? I can't run away again."

"You don't have to do that either." He chuckles, wiping her tears. "There's only one thing you have to do right now."

"What's that?" She sniffs and shakes her head again. "I'm sorry, by the way. I swear I can go days, months even, without crying."

"Relax. Enjoy the moment."

With a deep breath and more sniffles, she goes on. "I know. I'm so torn. I don't know what I'm doing. I mean, lying here under the stars with you. It's the only place I want to be. But then, I think about my people back home, and I can't imagine life without them."

"Well." He pulls her close. She leans into him, face buried in his chest. "You don't have to make any decisions now, no plans. We can take it one moment at a time. Didn't you say you barely know when you have to be at work?" She nods into his chest. He smooths her hair, resting his hand on her neck. "Then why are you trying to figure out your whole life right now?"

"The stuff I'm talking about means a lot more to me than some crappy job at a crappy bar."

"That's good to hear." He laughs and kisses the top of her head.

"How are you always so calm?" she asks after several moments of silence. Sitting up, she rubs her eyes and temples. He snorts a quick laugh, thinking of the emotional roller coaster he's been on for the last two days.

"I'm better at hiding it than you, that's all." He cups her soft, tear-moistened cheek in one hand, catching her eyes with his. "I love you, Amanda. I have since the day we met. And if it hasn't changed in all the years you've been away, why would it now?" She blinks away tears and smiles, pressing her cheek into his hand.

"I love you too, Mike." Her words are quiet, but sure. There's no doubt in her eyes. His heart soars.

"That's all I need to know. Everything else will work itself out." He leans in and kisses her pouted lips. "But for now, we've got no place to be but here." She grins. And, reading his mind, begins unbuttoning her blouse.

Her tits are high and proud in the smooth sculpted cups of her black bra. She drops her shirt off her shoulders. Firelight glows on them. He moves in, pressing his face into the soft mounds, kissing the flat space between them.

She giggles and unclasps her bra. It slips away like magic. His face meets more soft, weighted flesh. He cups both breasts and kisses one and the other, squeezing and pressing them to his face. Her fingers run over his shoulder to his neck and up to his hair. She pulls at him, bringing his mouth to hers. Her fingers drag up through his beard. With a kiss hot and fervent, she bites at his lower lip. Together, they ease themselves back onto the blanket. She kicks off her sneakers as he rises up and pulls his shirt over his head.

"You should take your boots off this time," she teases.

"I should," he agrees, sitting up.

She's wiggling out of her jeans beside him. He watches her as he pulls at his laces, eyes gleaming. Her body is flawless in the warm, flickering light. A gentle breeze blows. Goosebumps form all over her golden lit skin.

Her dark, rosy nipples spring to life. He licks his lips, ready to taste her. Stretching out beside her, his bare feet hit the cool grass. On one elbow, he looks her over from his new angle. She's smiling up at him with eyes full of love.

"Look at you," he says, running his free hand over her belly to her fuzzy mound. "All naked and exposed. In the middle of nowhere. What am I going to do with you?" he asks, petting her all the while.

"I've got a few suggestions," she says, her eyes landing on his pants, still buttoned.

"Aren't you naked?" he asks, pinching the flesh under her fuzz.

"I suppose I am. Should I be quiet then?" she teases, rolling her hips under his hand. "I didn't realize we were still playing." She strokes his bare chest, looking with shameless eyes. "By all means." She blinks once, slowly. "Shut me up." A brazen taunt.

"You're awfully bold, considering your current situation." He runs his hand over her belly and chest, resting it at the base of her throat. Her eyes narrow. Her cheeks flush. He feels her breath quicken under his palm.

"Are you threatening me?" she asks, eyes still locked on his.

"You're testing me," he says, his voice low, hand still resting on her throat.

"Am I?" She wears a smirk. "I thought I was a natural submissive," she mocks, her tone pulling at his loins, begging him to act. "I'm needing someone to...master me? Was it?" Every movement, every word drips with their mutual desire.

He holds her gaze as his hand slips over her throat to hold her chin. It's dainty. He eases it from one side to the other. She stares with sultry eyes, silently goading him on.

She licks her lips and writhes with each breath. Their sexy banter demands that he act. It's his move and she's waiting.

***

The fire crackles beside her. Sparks fly all around. Mike holds her face. His stony eyes give little away. *Did I go too far?* she wonders, anticipating his next move. She's burning inside, waiting for more, yearning for his strong hand to guide her. To make her crumble at his feet and beg for more. He brushes his thumb over her lower lip, pulling it away from her teeth. He parts his lips to speak. She hangs on the moment, breath caught in her chest, cheeks hot, waiting... He squeezes, squishing her mouth into a fish face. A smile cracks and his eyes crinkle at the corners. "Not tonight, my love." He laughs a hearty laugh and gives her face a gentle shake.

"You're a dick," she says through squished lips before pushing his hand away. Blushing again, she sits up, pulling her knees to her chest. "Not funny, Mike," she shouts, letting her disappointment show.

"Come on." He laughs again, sliding up beside her. "I'm sorry." His arm rests on her shoulder. "It didn't feel right, to be honest." He nudges while he's talking. "You know what I mean?'

She looks at his smiling face. His eyes twinkle like the stars above. "I guess," she says, still pouting. "But you're still a dick." She smiles and relaxes into his embrace.

"Come here," he says, pulling her onto his lap, cradling her in his arms. Their faces are inches apart. He's holding her chin again, speaking softly. "*This* feels right. Doesn't it?" He kisses her. "I don't want to play games." Another kiss. "Not here, not tonight." She melts in his arms.

His words are more than enough for her injured ego. "I only want to love you tonight."

His lips are soft and warm against hers. She gives in completely, wrapping her hands around the back of his neck. She slides her tongue between his parted lips. He squeezes her shoulder as his tongue darts over hers. His other hand runs up her bare thigh.

A jolt of pleasure courses through her as he reaches her moistened slit. With his thumb, he strokes her pubic hair. His fingers work magic on her labia as he presses the arch of his hand into her clit. Denim, stretched tight over his growing cock, is rough against her bare ass. Rolling away from his skilled touch, she sits on her knees in front of him. Unbuttoning his jeans, he wiggles awkwardly out of them. With a toss, they join hers in the grass.

She settles onto her feet, giggling. His messy hair and eager grin pull at her heart. His naked cock, rigid in the firelight, pulls at something more base.

Bending over it, she nudges with her nose, brushing the silky smoothness against her cheek, her mouth waters. Her insides pulse. He lets out a grateful moan when she sucks the tip into her mouth. His hand strokes her inner thigh, teasing her dripping parts.

She cups the warm, velvet skin of his balls, rolling them in her palm. Relishing the fullness in her mouth, she bobs her head up and down.

The cool night air tickles her exposed sex. He pulls at her. She sits up, guided to meet him chest to chest. Straddling his outstretched legs, their centers meet. He's as hard as stone. She's wet and yielding. It's like the first time. Heated skin pressed together. Her arms and legs wrap around him. She clings and rocks as his hands clutch her shoulders.

Their mouths search each other's faces, necks, and ears. Hungry coos and desperate sighs fill the air as pulsing pleasure mounts. His beard scratches her face and neck as she rides to delirium. Strong, coarse hands stroke her back to earth. She opens her eyes. His are there, bright and sparkling.

"Make me cum," he pleads.

She eases off him and lowers herself again to put her mouth on him. The taste of her juices on his cock is strange but enticing. She sucks it clean and takes it all in her mouth. Pumping it in and out of her throat, she breaks for air. Her hand glides over the length of his shaft as she sucks at the tip. His body tenses. He squeezes at her waist.

Bitter, sweet, and salt fill her mouth. He groans with appreciation and falls back onto the ground. Amanda crawls alongside him, curling in his arms. The fire warms her back, his body, her front. Safe and contented, she whispers, "I love you." The words have never felt so right.

"I love you too." He tightens his embrace.

They doze, quiet and peaceful as the night hums around them. The full moon glows. She watches the sky as Mike's breath grows heavy with sleep. *Can it really be this easy?*

Years alone, wondering where he was, what he was doing. How many nights had she dreamed of these arms? How many times had she questioned her choices? And here they are, under the stars. Professing their love as if she had never left.

After only two days, she's willing to give up the life she's built. *What would it be like to crawl into bed with him every night? To wake with him beside me every morning? The troupe would be fine without me. They could find someone to take my place. But how would I do without them? Could I do it? Could I really walk away from them all? Could I leave Chicago and performing and never look back? Will he still want me once he learns what really happened? Will he still love me?*

Her thoughts keep her from relaxing. She rolls toward the flames, watching them flicker and twist as quiet tears roll down her cheeks. Mike's arm rests under her neck. Sitting up, she turns to admire his sleeping face, wiping at her cheeks.

She watches the rise and fall of his chest. His hand twitches. Never has she seen him so bare. Lying naked under the sky, fast asleep. Without even a blanket. She wants to kiss his parted lips, to stroke his beard, to lay her cheek on the soft hair of his chest. But she doesn't want to disturb him either. Instead, she stands, pulling the blanket over him.

The softly moving river calls her restless soul. It rolls along, reflecting the moon. A cool breeze lifts her hair from her neck. She stretches her arms above her head and breathes in the sweet, muddy air. Moving naturally through her favorite yoga poses, she finds some peace.

***

Mike's feet are cold and wet. He opens his eyes to the starry sky. Glowing embers and tiny flames whisper. The damp quilt is empty beside him. Rising up on his elbow, he spots Amanda. She's naked on the river's edge, stretching and luminous in the silver moonlight. He watches for a moment, appreciating her form. Her presence is a gift in itself. To see her embrace this space, his space, with such intimate joy is beyond what he imagined. There's a purity in her movement, a grace in her silent surrender. He's spellbound.

"I didn't want to wake you," she says, looking his way with a smile.

"Thanks." He sits up, looking for his pants.

"Wait." She hurries back to the blanket. "Come, be naked with me."

He raises an eyebrow and scratches his beard. "Didn't we just do that?" he teases, standing up and shaking his jeans out.

"Come on," she pleads, taking his jeans from him, dropping them back on the ground. With his hands in hers, she steps back, leading him to the riverside. "Stand here with me." She grins and turns away, pressing her back against his chest. Her skin is cool. He wraps his arms around her. She places her hands on his. They stand together. The river flows. The moon shines. He squeezes. She sighs. Time is irrelevant. Everything except their bodies and the nature that surrounds them is irrelevant.

"This is nice," he says, kissing the top of her head.

"Mmm," she responds, leaning into him even more. Leaves rustle overhead as a strong breeze wraps around them.

"Should we head in?" he asks, shielding her as best he can from the cold.

"I suppose." They gather their things and head inside. Naked as children. Screen door banging behind them.

The cabin is forever changed by her presence. Together, they spread a fresh blanket over the bed. He turns on the bedside lamp and switches off the overhead light. As she slides between the sheets, the picture is complete. His dreams are real.

She smiles up at him. "So, why did you bring me here?" she asks as he joins her under the blankets. "For real?"

"I told you already. To chain you to my woodstove."

"I'm serious, Mike. You've never had anyone here. Not even your parents. Why me?"

"I thought it was obvious." He looks at her, his smile gone. His chest tightens as she waits for more. "I wanted you to see my future. Wanted you to know what life could be like with me."

Her smile remains, though she blinks away emotional tears. "I'm not sure what to say…" Her words trail off as she looks away.

"Don't say anything." Her reaction feels like a punch in the gut. He smiles to cover. "We already talked about it. We're here now. That's what matters."

"Yes," she says, pulling his arm around her and snuggling into his chest. "I do love it here, with you." He relaxes with her words, holding her tight. "Thank you for bringing me here. It means a lot."

"I'm glad you like it," he says, stroking her shoulder. The silence growing between them is more awkward than he'd like. He can only imagine the turmoil in her mind. Wishing yet again he could unsay words. He turns off the bedside light and settles beneath her.

"Good night, Amanda."

"Good night."

His eyes need no time to adjust. The moon's light fills his tiny cabin. Everything is as it's always been. Except for the warm body next to his.

He kisses her face and buries the angst deep down, welcoming the solace of a dreamless sleep.

Chapter Twelve

Is every bird on earth singing? Amanda wonders, stepping out into the gentle morning light. Her bare feet tiptoe through dewy grass. Mike's t-shirt skims the top of her thighs. The smooth cotton caresses her skin. Her night had been restless. Dreams of harried show nights with missing costumes and missing music, running here and there backstage in strange theaters. Her friends all calling from different directions. Her, not being able to find them. She'd woken several times in a panic. Mike's weight beside her was calming. Then, falling back to sleep, to more confusing dreams. But the unease made for a long night of waking and wondering. She'd talked to her parents, her mom, young and vibrant, her dad madly in love. They'd sat together at their old kitchen table. Their words lost somewhere between the pillow and the night. Even Aunt Betty had made an appearance, clucking her tongue and shaking her head at Amanda running naked through dark backstage passages.

She shakes her head, rubbing the fragments of dreams from her eyes. With a deep breath she surveys her surroundings. The magic of sunset has been replaced by sparkling morning dew and beckoning wildflowers. She walks along the tall grass, pausing to appreciate the array of colorful blossoms. Yellow, white, pink, and purple pop up over the feathery grass. They smell so sweet, so real. Not like the potted plants of Chicago's city streets. Clovers and dandelions play at her feet as she sniffs at various flowers. There may not be answers here. But there is peace. She breathes it in.

The screen door squeaks and slams. She turns. Mike's standing at the top of the steps, in only jeans, her favorite way to see him, casual and confident, his strength on display. He smiles at her, running his hand over his face and beard. "Good morning." His voice, a cheery complement to the singing birds.

"'Morning," she chimes, her heart glowing with joy.

If she could design her own heaven, it would look a lot like this. "I didn't want to wake you. Everything is so beautiful out here. I want to take it all in." She crosses the wet grass to where he stands. He steps down off the stairs and wraps her in his arms. With her cheek against his chest, she breathes deeply, wishing the moment could last forever.

"All I got here is beer and coffee. Are you interested in either?" His voice, still rough from sleep, rumbles in her ear.

"I could be sold on some coffee, and maybe some water?"

"Now you're just being difficult." He chuckles and squeezes her tight before letting her go.

She follows him in and climbs back into bed, wrapping herself in the quilt. The smell of dust, old wood, and countless fires in the stove surround her. She listens as Mike starts the coffee.

How can something so new feel so much like home? She curls up and stretches out again. As she waits on Mike, she reads through the titles of books on his shelf. There are hunting and survival guides, some classics like Thoreau and Jack London, and a dozen or so paperback pulp fictions.

Amanda closes her eyes and imagines Mike stretched out, reclining on his bed, bare chested, reading one of those old paperbacks. She feels the morning's sun on her face and sees herself in the scenario, curled up on the loveseat, sipping coffee, peeking at him from behind her own book.

"What's this?" Mike asks as he approaches the bed holding the collar she bought the day before, mischief all over his face. Amanda feels her own face go red in an instant. She pulls the blanket over her head.

"I lied," she says through the cover. "It's your surprise. It's stupid."

"I don't think so." His tone shifts. He kneels on the end of the bed. "Let's try it on," he coaxes, tugging gently on the blanket. She peeks out, cheeks still blazing.

"What were you doing looking through my stuff?"

"I was looking for toothpaste." He pulls on the blanket some more. "Let's see how it looks." She's still in his t-shirt and feeling vulnerable. The collar in Mike's hand is a symbol of her submission. The fact that she bought it, even more so. But the sight of the leather and the subtle shift in his voice causes a reaction deep inside her that she can't deny.

"Okay." His shirt slips over her head with ease.

"Good girl." He smiles and holds it out, beckoning to her. "Now, come here. Let me put it on you." She crawls to him.

With gentle hands, he brushes her hair to one side and slides the collar around her neck, with a jingle. "Sit up, my pet." She does what his saccharine tone demands. The birds are muted by the blood rushing in her ears. "Very nice. It suits you." Her cheeks bloom with his praise. She smiles and bats her eyes. He smooths her hair. "I'm sorry to say, I am terribly unprepared for this. I don't have a single toy for you." He stands up and crosses his arms over his chest, stepping back to admire her. "And look at you, so perfect." A haze of desire blots out her peripheral vision. The moment is absurd, but no less enticing. He scans the room for inspiration. She watches, silent.

"I know." He grins and steps closer to her. Stroking her hair and face, he speaks softly. "Lie down. I'll be back." Again, she does as she's told. Curling up like a cat in the sun, she closes her eyes and wonders what's to come. The door slams shut. *Funny how something as simple as a dog collar could change everything in an instant. His whole demeanor changed and I followed suit. What sort of psychology is going on here? Fuck Thoreau. Where are the books by Freud?* Amanda chuckles to herself as she hears the door open and close again. Some rummaging in the kitchen and Mike is back. She looks up to see him placing a dish on the floor. He pulls a chair close to the dish.

"You asked for water." His eyes smile as he settles onto his chair.

Are you fucking kidding me? She looks over the rough wooden floor to the tin plate full of water. She glares with disdain. As she opens her mouth to protest, he holds up a finger.

"Wait. Before you speak, don't forget whose idea this was. Who went and bought herself a pretty little collar?"

She raises an eyebrow, considers telling him what he can do with the collar, but finds herself more curious than proud. *What will he do next? How can he make this tin plate on the floor sexy?* She closes her mouth and sits up on her knees. Dropping her hands to the floor, she glares at him. His eyes crinkle with delight.

"Good girl," he coos. Her knees follow as she crawls toward him. The floorboards are cleaner and smoother than they appear. "Come on, I know you're thirsty."

The dish rests at his feet. Kneeling in front of it, she lowers her head to sip the water. It's ice cold and tastes like pennies. "No. Not like that. Lap it up." He pushes his chair back and watches as she dips her head again, slowly lapping at the cool water. "Very nice. So obedient." Again, the internal battle goes on. Her pride wants to stand up and dump the water over his head. But curiosity and desire win.

She drinks her fill and sits back on her feet.

"I like this." He pauses, flips the small metal heart that dangles from her throat. "I think we'll change the rules. From now on, *this* is what makes you mine. When you wear it, you do as I say." Amanda nods her agreement, with her eyes closed. She relies on his words for direction.

"You learned something about desire the other night. Today, you'll learn about submission. Look at me, Amanda." Her eyes flash open at the sound of her name. "How does it feel to drink at my feet, on your knees, in the dust?"

She has a dozen snarky answers. But none of them find her lips. She only blinks and raises her chin.

"You're too good at this already," he says, leaning forward. "There's a freedom in submission, isn't there? When you submit, you are no longer responsible for anything. Except pleasing your master." He reaches out to stroke her hair. "I'm impressed. I thought for sure you'd put up a fight. Don't think I didn't see it. Hell, I could practically hear your thoughts when you saw the dish on the floor."

Amanda blinks again and holds his gaze.

"I have something else for you." She smiles. "But first, I want you to turn around." She does. "Now put your face on the floor." She does. "Raise your hips for me and spread your knees."

The floor is cold against her cheek and hard under her knees. With her head turned, she can see him watching her with a stone face. His hand strokes her backside. "I like you in this light." His words and his hand are like honey. Her body responds to both. She begins to wag her hips under his touch. He pulls away and leans back.

Swollen, she's eager for any contact he'll give. "Be still," he says as he begins stroking her again.

His fingers dance, feather-light around her most sensitive places. She fights the urge to back into it, to grind against any part that touches her. With her face firmly on the smooth floor, she closes her eyes. Heat springs from his fingers as they float over her delicate skin. She's still, but dripping.

"I wonder, have you ever been this wet before?" He runs a finger down her thigh, wiping away her juices. He chuckles. "Sit up, Amanda." She does. "Now, turn around and come back to me." She crawls back to him, eyes glazed.

"Open your mouth." She parts her lips, still focused on the aching between her legs. Mike brings his hand to her mouth and slides in a single, plump berry. "Taste it," he says.

The scent of ripe blueberry envelops her. Its juice bursts in her mouth, so fresh and sweet. It's the most delicious thing she's ever tasted. He feeds her several more, one at a time. She's delirious, her senses heightened. With the sweetness of the berries and the aching deep in her cunt, she's forgotten where the ceiling is. It's madness. She looks at Mike, pleading with desperate eyes. He smiles and lifts her into his arms. Crossing the room, he places her on the bed. She melts onto the mattress, weak with longing, relishing the sensation of her legs finally together. She wriggles.

"Don't give up yet, my dear." The song in his voice is infuriating and intoxicating at once. "I'm not finished with you. Sit up." She does as she's told. He undoes the button on his jeans and pulls the zipper down. She sighs at the sight of him, exposed, yet not fully erect. "Show me what you can do."

She grins and takes the full soft flesh in her mouth. The taste of blueberries still on her tongue, it mingles with his sweet, musky scent. Moaning, she pulls him deeper in her mouth, tingling all over. He's hard quickly, prodding the back of her throat.

"Lie back," he breathes.

Holding her knee to her chest, he enters her from the side. She squeals, ecstatic and panting. Tiny earthquakes erupt from her core, rippling to her toes and fingertips. His hands find her nipples, her clit, her tender ass.

"No one can hear you out here." He pinches her nipple, hard. She screams, releasing everything she's been holding back. Primal sounds escape, shocking her, goading him on. He's pumping harder, gripping her knee. She moans through cascades of glee, her body pulsing.

***

The sound of her cries, her absolute abandon... It's the ultimate reward for his efforts. She's beyond putty, and all for him. Mike watches as her tits and ass bounce with each driving thrust. Her cheeks are red, her eyes closed. He squeezes one fleshy part and moves on to another, leaving red fingerprints as a trail to his favorite places. He pulls out and drags her by her hips to the edge of the bed. She gasps and searches his face.

"Up on your feet. Bend over." She does as she's told. He quickly returns to the soft wet heat of her sex. Muffled moans rise from her face in the bed. Squeezing her hips, he drives deeper still, pumping to his throbbing elation.

Amanda sighs and wiggles free, dropping in a heap on the bed. He sits beside her and gently removes the collar. Her face is buried under tousled hair.

"All that over some blueberries," she mumbles with a weak laugh.

"Yeah. Blueberries," he responds with a laugh of his own. "I'm keeping this," he says, shaking the collar and tossing it on the sofa beside the bed.

"It's yours." She gives a wave of dismissal and pulls the blankets over her shoulder, rolling away from him and off to sleep.

This woman. It's all he can think. Lounging naked beside her, spent. His life will never be the same. That's a certainty. But how? How can he get her to stay? Spending days without her, let alone weeks or months even. The thought is simply too much. He stands up and gets dressed, boots and all.

Moments later, the wildlife busies itself with no regard to Mike or his troubles. His boots crunch along a worn path. *How can I let her go? How can I make her stay?* He laughs in spite of himself.

She may submit willingly in his bed. But never in life. The tapping of a woodpecker calls his attention. He looks toward the sound, narrowing his eyes. Its blazing red head bounces in a spiral around the trunk of a nearby tree. It pays him no mind. Gray squirrels titter above him, bouncing from branch to branch. His mind follows suit, bouncing from joy to dread and back. Amanda sleeps in his bed on the other side of the trees. She's there and it's real. No dreams or memories. It seems indecent to remember her as she used to be. But the mind does what it will.

He's a fourteen-year-old boy again, following her along another worn path beside the river. It's similar to his current surroundings, but dirtier. "People are so gross," Amanda said, sneering at an old diaper. "I mean, why would you even bring a baby down here?"

"I'm sure it was brought here by the flood, or maybe an animal."

"Ech. However it got here, it's still gross. Someone had to throw it out somewhere."

"You're right."

"Hm. Look at this," she says, pushing through some overgrown brush.

"What?" he asked as she stepped aside. "Hobo camp," he said with an air of worldliness.

"This is worse than the diaper." She laughed. "Could you imagine sleeping here?" She gestured to the stained old mattress beside a blackened firepit. Broken glass and charred tin cans littered the area around it.

"Not really."

"I get the whole hobo thing. I guess. Always wondered what it would be like to hop on a train and ride away." Her voice trailed off, her eyes on the wind in the trees. He should have known then that she wouldn't stick around. "But this…" She nodded at the dirty mattress. "Well, it's a bit too real. Me and Betty may not have much, but at least my bed is clean." She giggled and marched on through the clearing.

"You really think you could do that?" he called after her. "Just hop on a train." She turned to look at him. "That's kinda stupid, you know."

"You're kinda stupid." She had laughed when she said it. But Mike could still remember the anger in her eyes. "Let's go," she said with a bite that still stung.

Funny, he thinks, *how powerful hindsight can be.* It was obvious that day and countless others how unhappy she was. He had been so smitten, so happy in her presence that he never even noticed. He'd always assumed that she was as happy as him.

THUMP.

"What the…" Mike's blind ambling had led him to a fallen tree across the familiar trail. "Well shit. There's something to do." He'd never worn helplessness well. And helpless seems to be a theme when it comes to his feelings for Amanda.

***

Amanda dozes in the sunny cabin, snuggled into the gentle calm that surrounds her. A distant crack of an axe hitting wood startles her. *Does he ever stop working?* She rolls onto her back, staring at the cracks on the ceiling. *I bet this place will be amazing once he owns it.* For a moment she allows herself to paint that picture with herself in it. "Maybe someday," she says. Standing up, she searches the room for her clothes. They're piled beside the door with her shoes.

Outside, she follows the sound of Mike's axe. He's standing over a fallen tree, sweat soaking through his t-shirt, swinging away like John Henry. The sun filters through leaves, and branches speckle the ground with its light. He looks up mid swing. Their eyes meet. He smiles. With a cracking blow the tree splits in two.

"That thunderstorm the other day must have knocked it down." He nods toward the tree. Then, bending down, he grips a branch of the smaller upper half and hefts it off the trail. Stepping over the brush, he drops it onto the ground.

The man is moving trees here.

He steps behind what remains of the tree. "You might want to step back a bit." Chips of bark fly as his axe makes contact. The muscles of his arms stretch and bunch with his rhythmic swings. His eyes focus on the trunk. A quarter of the way through, he stops. "I'll be done with this before too long. Then we can figure out our food situation."

"I'm fine." She shrugs and leans against a nearby tree.

Looking on, she appreciates the wildlife. Ferns and thorny bushes fill the spaces beneath the trees. Everywhere is green, with the occasional patch of purple, white, and yellow flowers. Mushrooms as big as her hands grow on the sides of the trees. The bugs buzz near her face. Gnats become too comfortable with her presence. She swats them away from her face.

"I'm going back," she says over his chopping. He looks up and smiles, nodding.

There's a cloud around her face before she reaches the clearing. *Not sure if I could ever get used to the bugs.* They aren't as bad in the sun.

She walks to the river and settles herself in the grass. The sparkle of the sun on the water reminds her of sequins under stage lights. She sighs and wonders what's happening at home. Cindy has most likely torn apart her costume to rebuild it. She's never satisfied. Jessica has probably chosen a new song to dance to, again. She can never settle on one thing. Jonathan is writing a script that no one would ever see in his tattered notebook.

But who is she kidding? No one is awake yet. Except maybe Bridgette. She and Amanda are always the first to wake up. They are usually well into their second pot of coffee before anyone else stirs.

She misses Bridgette most of all. *What would she say about all this? What sage advice would she offer?* She laughs at the thought that someone so much younger than her has become such a sound influence in her life. She thinks of the many conversations they've had over the years. *How have I kept Mike a secret all that time? Surely, I mentioned him before.*

Right on cue, he steps into the clearing, axe in hand, glistening with sweat. *He could do the best lumberjack routine,* she thinks with a little giggle. *But, he would never. He takes himself too seriously.*

"What are you smiling about?" he asks, approaching her.

"Nothing really. Picturing you on a stage somewhere."

"Huh." He chuckles. "Good luck with that." He lays the axe on the table and peels his shirt over his head, wiping the sweat from his face and chest with it.

"That's what I'm talking about," Amanda cheers, leering at him as he squints into the sun.

"Very funny. Did you find the blueberry bush?" he asks, looking down at her.

"No." She shakes her head.

"Come on then," he offers his hand. She takes it and is lifted to her feet with ease. He leads her behind the cabin. Growing against the wall is a huge bush loaded with berries. Like a child, she starts plucking the ripe berries and popping them in her mouth. They aren't as overwhelmingly delicious as the one he had fed her earlier. But they are sweet and juicy.

Mike picks a handful and pours them into his mouth. Then he walks toward the trees. Amanda follows, with several berries in her hand. He pulls at a limb, revealing tiny, bright red apples. He tugs a couple free and pulls a knife from his pocket. With smooth, fluid motions he quarters the small fruits and removes the seeds. The slices are dwarfed by his hand as he offers her a piece. She takes one and bites through the crisp skin. It's tart compared to the blueberries, but delicious just the same. He offers more. She takes another slice.

"I feel like I'm in the Garden of Eden." She laughs.

"Does that make me the snake?"

"You are pretty good at tempting me," she says with a smile, admiring his sculpted chest and shoulders. A tingle runs up her spine and back down to her aching nethers. Her stomach growls audibly. She snickers. "But unless you have a bacon bush or a pancake tree around here somewhere, we better talk about some real breakfast."

"You're right." His eyes crinkle with a smile. "We should head out. I should have planned better."

"Yeah. I'd love to stay longer, but I'm starving." She rubs her belly. "And this fruit is making me hungrier."

"Me too."

"Is that diner still open? The one we used to go to all the time, down the street from my house?" she asks on a whim of nostalgia. "They had the best pancakes."

"Yep. You wanna go? It's not far from here, really."

"Yes. Next time you bring me here, you have to remember to bring food."

Chapter Thirteen

Next time. She had said it, hadn't she?

Mike watches her load her coffee with more cream and sugar than any sane person could possibly enjoy. "At what point does it cease to be coffee and become coffee-flavored milk?" he teases.

"I like sugar," she retorts, laying her spoon on the table. The old farmers are sitting around a large table talking politics and crops. Amanda sits, sipping her coffee, reading her menu.

Next time. He's holding on to those two words and the hope they give him. He knows she's happy with him. He knows she's enjoying their time together. What he doesn't know is if it will be enough. If he will be enough. Before she'd come back, he was confident. He had plans and goals, and was right on track for achieving them. But now, as he watches her from across the table in the booth they used to frequent, he's anything but confident.

"Well hey there, handsome." Krystal, a waitress who's been serving him breakfast for years, leans against the booth and lays her hand on his shoulder. "Haven't seen you in a while. Where ya been?" Her voice is full of gravel and cheer.

"'Morning, Krystal. I've been busy."

"I can see that," she says with an exaggerated wink at Amanda. "Are you here for food or just the coffee?"

"Here for the food, and the service," he flirts, looking at Amanda. "You ready?"

"Are you?" Amanda asks.

"I know what he's getting, honcy. How 'bout you?"

"I'll get the cheese omelette with pancakes," she says, handing her menu to Krystal.

"The usual?" Krystal asks Mike, taking his unopened menu.

"You know it," he says with a wink.

"This one's trouble," she says to Amanda, a slight blush on her wrinkled face.

"Don't I know it," Amanda responds, her sparkling eyes on his. He wonders what dirty thoughts are behind those eyes.

Krystal watches them for a brief moment, then says, "It shouldn't be too long." Mike gives her a nod but maintains eye contact with Amanda.

"So, what are we going to do today?" she asks, a smirk playing at the corners of her lips.

"What do you want to do?" His tone makes no secrets of his intentions.

She smiles and lets out a slow, low giggle. "Actually," she responds, "I thought we might walk around a bit. For old times' sake." She shakes her head, still smiling. "It doesn't look like it's changed much."

"It hasn't," Mike answers, wondering what his next move should be. His goal is to convince her to stay. That she doesn't have to go back. But, how? How can he make her see that she would be happy here with him? Happy, yet still independent. *Betty's house?*

"Mike?" Amanda says.

"Sorry, I was lost in thought there."

"I could see." She narrows her eyes. "About what?"

"I'm wondering how I'm going to get you to stay."

She pulls back, forcing a smile with sad eyes. "Mike…"

Krystal appears at their table, breakfasts in hand. "Need anything else?" Mike looks at Amanda. She shakes her head.

"I think we're good. Maybe some more coffee when you get a chance."

"Thank you," Amanda says.

"All righty, enjoy." Krystal disappears, leaving them alone with their steaming plates. It smells and looks amazing, but suddenly Mike's not hungry. He's hanging on whatever words Amanda was about to say.

She smiles fully and picks up her fork. "I'm starving, and this looks delicious." She begins dressing her pancakes, showing no interest in continuing their conversation. Maybe he was foolish to say it. But what does it matter? She'll never know how much she means to him if he doesn't say it. Hunger overcomes the turmoil in his heart. They eat quickly, saying little.

Krystal clears the plates and refills their coffee, making herself scarce. He sighs heavily and sips the scalding coffee. "I have a confession."

"Oh?" Amanda asks, with a tilt of her chin.

"It's serious, Amanda."

"Oookay." She lowers her spoon to the table.

"Let's go." He pulls some bills out of his wallet and lays them on the table, sure it's more than enough. "Thanks, Krystal," he says over his shoulder as the bell on the door jingles.

Outside, the heat is thick and the sun shines off car windows and storefronts. They walk away from the diner. "So, when you left." He pauses, gauging her response. A slight flinch at the mention of her leaving. She's looking straight ahead, hands in her pockets. "When you left, I started helping your aunt Betty with yard work and stuff. I mean, I'd always helped you do it. It didn't seem right to stop because you left." She's walking beside him, shoulders rigid. "I'd stop by once a week, cut the grass, shovel the walk, whatever she needed. When I went to school, I got my brothers to do it. Anyway, when she passed away…" He pauses again. They are standing in front of Betty's house. Amanda stares at the porch. "She left me the house and everything in it. You and your dad were her nearest living relatives. She would have done anything to keep it out of his hands."

The color drains from her face. She looks at him, stunned.

"I've got a neighbor kid that I pay to do the yard work now." She turns away without a word and pushes the gate open. "I haven't changed anything inside." He follows. "Hell, I haven't even been inside for over a year. I couldn't bring myself to sell it. Part of me is sure this was her way of leaving it to you."

"She wouldn't leave anything to me," she says over her shoulder. "I want to go in." Her voice flat. "Alone."

Mike hands her the key from his key ring. She takes it and heads up the stairs of the porch. He sees her shoulders rise and fall with a heavy sigh. The key clicks in the lock. She disappears through the door. As a sense of dread settles over him, he scans the yard, looking for something to do.

***

Dank. It's dank inside. Amanda's shadow remains still in the light cast by the open doorway. The threadbare carpet is faded with age. It had been barely green the day she left. All the color appears to have worn away. The floorboards are peeking through at her feet. With an unsteady hand, she reaches for the light switch. The living room is unchanged. An enormous portrait of Jesus standing among a flock of sheep hangs above the vintage, floral print couch. The powder blue wingback recliner sits next to it. Crocheted doilies lie on the back and armrest as they always have. They're browned with age and years of cigarette smoke. Someone has cleaned the ashtrays. Amanda remembers them, always full of butts and ashes.

In a daze, she crosses to the couch and sits. A puff of dust rises around her. The blinds are pulled down. The room feels like a forgotten attic. She looks from the faded curtains to the wall of old family portraits in heavy metal frames. All people she'd never known, from a time when her family wasn't such a waste of space.

The table lamp casts a dim light from its heavy maroon shade. The beaded fringe hangs limp with years of dust. Amanda sinks farther into the cushion, staring at the fringe. She remembers a night years before. She hadn't thought of it in so long. It had begun to feel more like a bad dream than a memory.

Her dad, smelling of whiskey, took her from her bed in the middle of the night. He wrapped her in her blanket and carried her outside, laying her in the backseat of the car. "Shh, baby girl. It's all right. Go back to sleep." He tucked her pillow under her head and handed in her favorite teddy bear. The door shut. He climbed into the front seat. The engine started. As he backed out of their gravel drive, the metal of his flask caught the light from the streetlamp.

With the trust only a naive, young girl can have in her father, she closed her eyes and drifted back to sleep. His flask had been a mainstay ever since Mama had gone. She dreamed of Mama that night. Of hanging clothes on the line and shelling peas on the front porch. They would sing and dance together, and tell stories. Each one more fantastical than the last.

Mama always had the best ones. When Amanda came home from school, Mama would be writing or painting with her old records playing. She'd always welcome her with a smile and a hug. She smelled like flowers and food. Then they would make dinner for Daddy. He was home every day at the same time, so happy to see his girls. They'd run into his arms. He'd smell of sweat and labor. So many smiles.

At dinner Mama would listen with rapt attention while Daddy talked about his day. Their eyes always full of love for each other. Amanda hadn't known how blessed she was. Their love shone like the golden light of sunset.

But Mama got sick. She lost weight. She lost hair. She cried a lot when she thought Amanda wasn't looking. Daddy worked more and grew quiet. The golden light of their love faded to something dark, something full of dread.

One day, Daddy stopped going to work. He stayed home and never left Mama's side. Amanda hovered around them, as close as she could. Daddy all but forgot her. But Mama would call to her from the queen-size bed. They'd lie together, the three of them, Mama in the middle. She'd hold them both in her frail arms.

She barely talked at that point, never told stories. Then it happened. As they lay, with only their breaths between them, Mama's stopped.

Daddy cried out, "No. No, no, no, no." He gathered her in his arms and sobbed. Amanda knew. Mama was gone.

She wrapped her small arms around them both and cried too. For two years Daddy tried. He tried to make their life normal again. He tried to be happy for her. But, in the end, whiskey and heartache won.

Amanda woke long after the car had stopped. Her dad had laid her on the couch. The same one she sat on now. He kissed her forehead and squeezed her tightly. She kept her eyes closed. He and smelly old Aunt Betty went into the kitchen. Cigarette smoke filled the air.

"I can't do it, Betty," he'd said, his words slurred. "She looks more like Mona every day. I can barely look at her sometimes." Amanda's heart broke. She knew what was happening.

"What are you going to do then, Jerry?" Betty asked, irritation evident. "Gonna drink yourself to death?"

"I don't know. But I know I can't do this. What happens when she gets older? When she becomes a woman? I don't know how to handle any of that. I'm not doing right by her now. I need time. I need time to sort it all out." There was silence.

Amanda lay there, waiting. Hoping he would change his mind and put her back in the car and take her home. She could hang the clothes and make dinner. She could make him happy again. Never as happy as Mama. But they could be happy again.

"All right, Jerry. I'll keep her. But you've gotta clean yourself up. And come back for her when you do."

"Thank you, Betty. I'll send money every month." With that, he left through the back door. He didn't say good-bye to his daughter who looked so much like her mother.

Sitting on the dusty, old sofa now, Amanda's cheeks are wet with silent tears. She wipes them away with the back of her hand and stands. Her aunt's room is to the right. It's of no interest to her. She'd rarely visited there. To the left is the kitchen and bathroom. The faded pink strawberries on the wallpaper greet her when she flips on the overhead lamp. It shines a dull light on a small table with two chairs. *This is where he gave me away.* She blinks away more tears.

Behind the stove are the stairs to her room. She recalls one of many nights hiding on those darkened stairs, listening to Betty on the phone, her cigarette smoke trailing up toward Amanda.

"What's your excuse this time, Jerry?" Silence. "She's been here for two years." More silence.

Amanda had shifted as quietly as possible, hanging on every silent pause. *Maybe he will ask to talk to me this time. It is my birthday. How long has it been since I've heard his voice?* "Well, you better get your shit together soon. I don't know how long I can afford to keep her. Haven't seen a check in a while." Silence again, a huff, and she hung up.

He didn't even ask to talk to me? Not even today? She left that night, snuck out the back door as soon as Betty had left the kitchen. She ran to Mike's house, wanted to throw rocks at his window, wanted to talk to him, to tell him that her dad missed her birthday, again.

From the sidewalk, she looked through his living room window. The lights were on. His whole family was there. Him, his mom, dad, and brothers all sat around together. She wished she knew what they were talking about, what they were watching on TV. She watched for a while, remembering her family, how happy they had been.

She couldn't knock. She couldn't join them. They'd call Betty for sure. Then she'd get it. Not for leaving, but for making Betty leave the house. Instead, Amanda went to the river. She sat on the beach and thought of diving in, of sinking to the bottom. *It would all be over then. No more pain. No more loneliness. Or would it be all pain and loneliness?*

What would she find at the bottom of the river? Who would miss her? Mike would. But he'd be better off without me. She remembers the water on her feet as it soaked through her shoes and socks. Her tears travel through time. Amanda chokes on her sob and turns away from the stairs.

The bathroom door stands open. She peeks around the corner. Aqua blue and mint green tiles still line the walls. She sees herself, the day she left for good.

Aunt Betty stood in front of her, blocking the door. "Well, you may have won yourself a golden ticket." Smoke trailing out with her words. Amanda grimaced in response, standing over the sink, watching for a pink line.

"That's a terrible thing to say, Betty," she replied, sure that her heart had stopped beating entirely.

"What do you mean? Getting knocked up by that boy is the best thing that could happen to you." She blew more smoke in her direction and waved her hand in dismissal before turning to leave her alone.

Amanda looked in the mirror, chest tight. *This isn't what I want. It's not what either of us want. He's always been my hero. But this? This isn't how it is supposed to be. He could never leave if I have his baby.*

Her reflection grew blurry as she questioned everything. Rocks filled her belly as she waited without breath. The first pink line showed dark and bold. Then, moments later, the second. It was faint, but surely there. The absolute last thing she wanted to see. She couldn't be. *Not now. Not like this. Mike's leaving for college at the end of summer. He'll never go now. I can't do that to him, to his family.*

Remembering that horrible day, now, on weak knees, she walks through the kitchen and up the stairs. Her head is filled with tar. At the top, her door falls open with a turn of the knob. Sunshine does little to warm the room.

A twin bed sits under the window, made the way she'd left it. The empty dresser hasn't a trace of the teenage girl who once lived there. The mattress squeaks as she sits down. She pulls at the lump under the blanket. It's the teddy bear she brought along from her real home. The stuffed animal she'd held and cried with more nights than she could count. Looking into its eyeless face, she remembers how she would twist them as a child. They fell off so often.

Her mom would take the button jar out of the closet and let her pick a new set of eyes. Then she would sew them on and kiss his face, and kiss her face.

Amanda's mouth opens, she wails. She sobs, clutching the worn and tattered bear to her chest and curling around it. The pain of years of neglect, of anguish, of loss, of running, of hiding from herself, from everyone. The feelings of worthlessness, of loneliness, of anger pour through her eyes, spit, and breath. She's in a million pieces, scattered over the years of silent misery.

Then, there are his arms around her. "Mike. I'm so sorry. I'm sorry I did it. I didn't want to. But I knew I had to. I had to. Please, don't hate me. Don't hate me," she begged.

Chapter Fourteen

Mike's leaning in the open doorway of the shed, staring at the collection of outdated tools, wondering if he shouldn't replace them. *Maybe she'll decide she wants to stay here. I'd help her fix the place up. Hell, we could gut it completely if she wanted. She could have it exactly the way she wants.*

He turns out to the yard, imagining what could be done with the space. It's bigger than he remembered it, plenty of sun. *She could have a garden. I could give her a job at the Speakeasy. Not that she'd need it. I'd take care of her, give her whatever she needs. If she lets me.* He's watching the house, waiting for her to come out. A lawn mower runs in a nearby yard. The smell of fresh-cut grass in the late morning sun is welcome in his weary mind. He settles against the doorway again, assessing the repairs the house needs. *If she doesn't want it, it's time to let it go. I can fix it up and make a nice profit.* The lawn mower stops. Birds are singing, and something else. It's faint, but Mike hears it. It's coming from the house. *Amanda.*

He's moving in an instant, crossing the yard to the back door. It's locked. "Damnit."

He can hear her cries through the door. His throat closes, his chest tightens. He hurries to the front porch. Inside, he follows her wails up the stairs to her old room. She's a pile of heaving sobs, clutching her ratty teddy bear. *What was I thinking? I never should have brought her here.*

"Amanda?" No response. "Amanda?" He steps into the room. She curls tighter around the bear. He's feeling completely helpless. Remembering all the silent tears she'd cried over the years for her lost mom, her absent dad, and her cold aunt, he does what he's always done.

Sitting beside her, he gathers her in his arms. She buries her wet face in his shoulder and continues to cry. Her tears soak his shirt.

The desire to take a bulldozer to the house and everything in it comes over him. He wants to run it to the ground and burn what's left. *What did they do to you?* He knows, rocking her, but thinks there are probably a ton of things she never told him.

She looks up, sobbing softly. "Mike. I'm so sorry. I'm sorry I did it. I didn't want to. But I knew I had to. I had to. Please, don't hate me. Don't hate me."

"What are you talking about? What did you do?" His heart pounds in his chest. "How could I hate you?"

"The baby. Our baby," she squeaks, as a new bout of sobs erupt from her chest. He goes cold all over. Numb with shock. She squeezes him. "I tried to tell you. I wanted to. I didn't know how. I didn't want to hurt you. I'm so sorry. I'm so sorry. I don't... I don't know what to do."

"Shh," he soothes. "It's okay. You're okay." It's not anger he feels, but something so much stronger. Disgust, rage, frustration, helplessness. In the flash of an instant he was given a family only to have it ripped away.

How could she do this to us? How?

"I didn't know what to do." Her voice is small and weak between whimpers.

"I'm going to go now." His words are calm, slow. "You're in no shape to ride on a motorcycle." He pulls his arms from around her. "I'm going to get the van. Then we can leave." He stands. She looks up, eyes pink, face red.

"I hate me too," she says softly and lies down with her teddy bear, closing her eyes.

"Fuck," he shouts as his bike fires to life with an angry kickstart. "What the fuck? How could she have done it?"

Tears burn in his eyes as he thinks of everything she stole from him. He rides fast and dangerously over the bridge. He thinks of his nieces and nephews. How he's watched them grow over the years, wondering what it would be like to have a son or a daughter of his own. He did. He had one and he never knew it. Was never given the slightest chance. His thoughts are cut off as he pulls into the shop. He'd forgotten what day it is, forgotten that they were still open. D approaches him, his mouth open to speak. "I don't have time for it today, D," Mike silences him as he walks by. He grabs the keys to

Amanda's van and heads out the door. "I'll be in tomorrow," he calls back to Jim.

Climbing in the van, he adjusts the seat. It smells of cigarettes and perfume. *This is what she did it for?* he thinks with disgust. Checking the rearview mirror, he sees his crew staring after him with puzzled looks. "Fuck this," he curses and heads back to that godforsaken house.

He finds her fast asleep in the small, flat bed. The worn blankets beneath her, the ratty bear clutched to her chest. Sitting at the foot of the bed, he watches her sleep. He looks around the sad little room. *She hated this life. No wonder she did it.*

He shakes his head, and the pain in his chest breaks free. He cries. He cries for the baby that never was, for the girl he loved whom he never really knew. He cries for Amanda, for himself, for all the years they've lost.

As the sun dips to the horizon, the room's one tiny window glows with the light of dusk. He sits in silence. "Hey," he says, softly, placing his hand on her leg. She doesn't stir. "Amanda." He gives her leg a little shake. Nothing. He stands and bends down, leaning over her face, his hand on her shoulder. "Hey." Her eyes flutter open. "Let's get out of here." She sits up, her brow crinkled, confusion on her face.

"Ohh," she cries, remembering what happened. She opens her mouth to speak.

"It's okay. We'll talk later. Let's get out of here."

***

She wakes, tucked neatly into Mike's bed. For a moment she wonders if it was all a dream. But she's fully clothed beneath the sheets. It all happened. Every delightful moment at the cabin. Every terrible one after that. *What was I thinking? What did I expect to find in that house?*

The fog of her emotional overload hangs heavy in her head. She thinks of Mike, of her painful confession. *What now? Is there anything left of us?*

Her lips are parched, and her head aches. She sits up and the room spins. With a shake of her head she stands and walks to the door. *I have to leave. I'm the last thing he wants to see.* She opens the door. It's quiet. The hall is dark. He's reading on the couch. "Hey," he says, looking up from his book as she enters the room.

"Hey." She offers a small smile and crosses to him. His face is full of concern. She sits opposite him at the end of the couch. Sitting upright, he lays his book on the coffee table. "Thank you," she says with trembling words, looking away from the tenderness in his eyes.

"For what?" he asks, placing a hand on her knee. She's surprised by this simple act of familiarity.

"For getting me out of there." She stares at his hand. It's thick and calloused, etched black with stains from years of work. She lays hers over his. It's pink and small in comparison. As she curls her fingers around his, tears form in her eyes again. *Why is he so good?* she wonders as they roll down her cheek. She blinks them away. Her mind is frayed. Her words get lost somewhere in her throat.

"But why?" she mutters.

Mike pulls her to him. She cries silently into his chest, thankful for him, for his strong arms and calm presence. He strokes her hair as her tears flow. "Don't you hate me?" Her breath shudders in her chest.

Squeezing her eyes against the tears, she commits it all to her memory. His arms around her. His breath in her hair. The crinkle of his eyes when he smiles. His voice. His hands. His body. She wants to hold every part of him in her mind. She has to remember him, exactly as he is. She wants to remember him before anger flashes in his eyes. Before he pushes her away.

"I'm sorry." Her words are muffled by his chest.

"It's okay. I understand." He's quiet. His hand rests heavy at the base of her neck. "I understand. I don't hate you." He breathes deep. "The problem is, I love you. I can't not love you. No matter how angry I am for what happened. I can't not love you."

She shudders against him.

***

"Will you come to bed with me?" Amanda asks, her eyes puffy and red. "I don't want to be alone." The tightness in his chest holds his joy hostage. This moment could be so different if he hadn't learned what he learned, hadn't brought the past back to them both. Oh how much happier he'd been not knowing.

"Okay." He stands and offers his hand. She takes it, looking down. They walk hand in hand to the bedroom and lie on the bed, fully clothed.

"Hold me, please." Her voice is tiny in the dark. He brings the blanket over them and pulls her as close as he can. She shudders under his arm.

What now? How can we fix this? He grapples with anger and guilt. *How could she do it? Why wasn't I there for her? Why didn't I figure it out? I could have stopped her.* Her hand rests on his; she's curled around his arm like she had been the teddy bear, clinging to him.

"It's going to be all right," he says, his lips against the top of her head. She's silent in response. Her body's relaxed. She didn't hear.

He shifts against her body and settles in for the night.

***

Amanda wakes in the night and slips out from under his arm. *I have to go. I'm a coward. But it's better this way. This way, he can't tell me to leave.* She remembers pieces of the afternoon, her painful confession, riding in the passenger seat of her van in silence, being led into the apartment. She pauses at the thought of his gentle guidance. *I don't deserve him. Surely, he doesn't want me anymore.* She finds a notepad on his desk and a pen and heads into the bathroom. With the door locked, she starts writing.

Mike,

I'm sorry

Her hand hovers over the paper. She hesitates, tempted to tear it out and throw it away, to climb back into bed with him and stay. To wait for the morning, when they've rested and he's had time to think about everything.

She should stay so he can have closure. So he can say everything he's sure to say. *He says he can't not love me. That doesn't mean he wants me anymore.* The thought of him letting her go… The tears return. Her heart aches in her chest. It's so much worse than the first time. It's surely the last time she'll see him. But this way, she won't have to hear his rejection. She'll never see the look of anger in his eyes when he tells her how he really feels. She can tuck the memories away and hold them close whenever she needs to. It's better this way. She tears the sheet out, shreds it, and throws it away.

Mike,
Thank you for everything. I have to go.
Always, Amanda

What's wrong with you? She looks in the mirror. Bloodshot eyes stare back. *He deserves more than this. You can't sneak out in the middle of the night. You may not want to face it, but this is your doing. You jumped in headfirst. Sure, he may have held your hand. He may have followed willingly, but you knew how this was going to end.*

She turns the faucet on and splashes cold water on her face.

On tiptoe, she slips into Mike's room. She gathers her things and brings them into the living room to pack up. Her phone is on the counter, dead. She'd left it behind the night before. Finding Mike's charger, she plugs it in and makes her way to the couch to settle in for the night.

It doesn't feel right to lie next to him anymore. She looks at his bookshelf. It's full of titles she doesn't recognize. Biographies, historical nonfictions, how-to's, some more classics. *Not a single self-help or romance novel in sight. I suppose he doesn't need them.* She runs her finger over the spines of the books on the nearest shelf. *I wonder if he's read them all?*

Ping. Ping. Ping.

Her phone jumps to life, jarring her, as several messages come pouring in at once. Amanda hurries to quiet it. Standing at the counter, she scrolls through the missed calls and messages from Chicago.

-Hey girl.-
-When you coming home?-
-Miss you, Bunny.-
-Come home already.-
-We've got to get ready for Friday?-
-Do we have your music?-
-Bunnnnnny?.?.-
-BTW, you got fired. Sorry.-
-When are you getting in?-

-We're doing rehearsals on Thursday night. You need stage time?-

She smiles and shakes her head. *God, I miss them.* For a moment, she forgets what's coming. She's looking forward to going home, to getting back on stage. But when she remembers what she's leaving behind, she's right back to confusion and pain. She types her response in a group text.

-Sorry for being MIA. Heading out first thing in the morning.-

Mike steps behind her, wrapping his arms around her waist. "You okay?" His forehead rests against the back of her head. She hits send quickly and sets her phone face down.

"Yeah," her voice cracks. "Restless, I guess."

"It really is okay, Amanda. I mean it hurts like hell. But I understand. You were a kid, you were scared. I get it."

She turns to face him, gratitude welling in her chest. "But aren't you angry with me? How can you be so gentle and understanding? I mean this is something that I've carried with me my entire adult life. I was so scared of what you would say, what you would do."

"Absolutely, I'm angry." He takes her hands in his. "I'm angry with every person who hurt you as a child. At everyone who raised you to think that was your only option. I'm angry with myself for being so oblivious to your pain. And I am angry with you for cutting me out completely. I don't know what I would have done back then, but I wasn't even allowed to mourn. Yes, I'm angry." He squeezes her hands. "But I forgive you. Because I love you, and now that you're back in my life I can't imagine living another day without you." He brings her hands to his lips and kisses each knuckle. His tongue sneaking out with each kiss, grazing her skin. She feels it all the way to her knees. *Don't do it,* she warns herself. *Tell him you're leaving.*

"Come back to bed?" His warm breath, followed by more kisses, melt her resolve.

Ping. Ping. Her phone calls to her. His sleepy eyes and soft lips win.

In his room, he holds her face in both of his hands. His lips find hers, slow and searching. Between kisses, his thumb caresses her lips. His fingers clutch her hair. She sighs, melting into him.

She brings her hands to his, presses her lips to the heel of his palm. His mouth is on her cheek, her ear, her neck.

"Amanda," he whispers.

One hand moves to the back of her head, the other to the small of her back. He pulls her closer, crushing her with urgency. Amanda shudders against his chest. Tears wet her eyes. But passion mounts. His body and desire eclipse her confusion. *One more time.* She runs her hand down his back.

He lets her go and slowly pulls her shirt over her head. She watches his silhouette as he does the same. A glorious moment when the heat of his bare skin meets hers. *If only this could last forever.*

He holds her close, his face against the top of her head. She breathes in his scent. Pulling away, he leaves her skin cold. His hands hold her arms as his lips inch down her neck and over her shoulder. His thumbs stroke her collarbones.

Her head falls back in surrender of his delicate kisses. They find her exposed throat, each one more tender than the last. His whiskers tickle along the way. Shivers follow those whiskers as he moves down her chest, between her breasts.

After his lips travel the length of her bare skin, he's on his knees before her. His hands move from her hips to the button of her jeans. While unbuttoning them, he kisses her exposed skin.

Unzipping, his kisses find her hairline. Warm breath engulfs her sex as he inches her jeans off her hips. She quivers as she steps out of each leg.

Mike's hands run over her calves, behind her knees, and up her thighs. His tongue slides into her slit, teasing her clit. She runs her fingers through his hair. Her breath catches in her throat. "Oh." A flush runs from his tongue to her cheeks. Her nipples stand erect, screaming for attention. One hand answers their call. The other holds her hip. She rolls onto his darting tongue. His other hand runs over the rise and fall of her breasts. "Oooh."

"Mmmmm." Mike's hands are back on her hips. His fingers dig in. He nudges her.

Two steps back and she's on the bed. A moment later Mike's there, beside her, naked. His cock prods at the soft flesh of her ass. His lips are on her shoulder, the back of her neck, her shoulder again.

With one hand, he trails from her waist to her thigh. He takes her knee and brings it toward her chest, opening her sex. His cock's thick head parts her lips, sliding in inch by inch. Each measured thrust reaches to her core. The pace of every smooth stroke begs her to stay. As pleasure courses through her, she's convinced that she could. He releases her knee. She pushes against him. His hand roams everywhere, like warm water spilling over her curves. The other holds her shoulder, pushing her forward. The slow grind quickens. Their bodies rock together. He squeezes at her shoulder and hip, pulsing inside her.

***

Amanda springs up as quickly as she can, and he hears the shower running before he can question what she is doing. He lies there, frustrated and confused. He'd noticed her bags in the living room. *Was she planning on leaving while I slept? Maybe, she was sure that I hated her. Of course she'd want to leave to avoid the confrontation. But, still? Even after I forgave her, assured her that it was okay?* He rolls over, staring at the wall. *No. She wouldn't. Not after everything we've shared. She wouldn't. Would she?*

He barely knows her now. As he considers it, he realizes even the girl he knew was erratic at best. *How could I really count on her?* His chest is heavy. Disappointment is imminent. Deep down he'd known it all along. But still…

The water stops. He waits. Moments pass. She doesn't return. He listens for her. Nothing. He stands up and grabs a pair of sweatpants from his dresser. She's sitting on the couch, phone in hand. Her hair is wet, she's wearing her own sweats and a tank top.

"What's up?" he asks, pausing in the hallway.

She looks up from her phone, eyes wide. "I thought you were asleep," she says, shifting in her seat, laying the phone face down on the couch beside her.

"Couldn't get there. What's going on, Amanda?" He stares directly at her. His patience is waning.

She looks away. Then, picks up her phone and fiddles with it some more. "I have to go," she says. Her eyes on the phone.

"I know. What's with this though?" he asks, gesturing at her bags, her phone in her hand. "It doesn't have to be this way. Sneaking out in the middle of the night?" His voice rises.

"I'm not sneaking," she shoots back. "I was waiting. I'm not sure what's going on. To answer your question. Not sure how to handle this. There are moments when I want nothing more than to stay, but then I think about home, and I just can't."

"What do you mean, you can't?" he asks sharply.

"I just can't, okay? I don't expect you to understand. *I* don't even understand. Everything in my life was going so well. Things were the way they should be. Then you came along. And…"

"What do you mean, *I* came along? *You* were the one who showed up *here*. *You* were the one who made yourself available. *You* were the one who called *me* for help. The list goes on, Amanda. *You* didn't have to be so damn…" He stops and stares at her.

"So damn what, Mike?"

"You. Amanda." His throat closes on her name.

She couldn't possibly understand what he means. Clearly, she doesn't feel the same way. He'd been a stop on her tour. A fling, a trip down memory lane. His lip twitches as he fights the words boiling his heart. The ones he could hurt her with. The ones that would make her feel the way he does.

"What?" she asks.

"I've said it already. It's always been you. But I was a fool to think that those words meant anything to you. You're incapable of putting anyone before yourself."

She's blinking away tears before he finishes his sentence. He flinches inwardly at the sight of them. Instant regret; he hates that she's hurting. He moves forward with a sigh and a shrug of his shoulders. The coffee table separates them.

"Look, I know neither of us asked for this. Maybe we should have seen the writing on the wall and went our separate ways at the start." He's looking down at her. "But we didn't. So here we are, tears and anger. History repeats itself. But now I know things I wish I didn't I know, things that will haunt me forever. It seemed doable when I thought you would be here with me. That we could grieve together and make things right. Maybe even…"

"What?" she asks, tears running down her cheeks.

"Never mind." He shakes his head. "I'm leaving. Take your time. I won't be back until you're gone." She closes her eyes and lowers her head as if she's looking at the floor. For a brief moment, he wants to gather her in his arms, to kiss away the tears, and push the world away. But he knows better. She's leaving and she won't be back. Time to face reality. He turns and heads back to his room to change.

He can't avoid her on his way out. She's sitting, silent, staring into the distance. He pauses at the door, hand on the knob, eyes straight ahead.

"It was great to see you again, Amanda. I mean that."

The door closes behind him. His shoulders slump.

He swallows the lump in his throat and heads down the stairs.

Chapter Fifteen

She has no more tears. Looking out the window at the still-dark sky she wonders, *Where did he go?* She paces from one end of the living room to the other. She goes out on the balcony. Looking down at the empty sidewalk, she thinks of him out there, walking alone. But he's not coming back. He said so. *No sense in waiting any longer.*

She gathers her backpack and suitcase and leaves his apartment. It's silent in the stairway. There's not a soul in the parking lot. Dehydrated and exhausted, she moves slowly, passing parked cars. She's alone. Her van sits near a streetlight. She unlocks the doors and throws her bags in the back. With a heaviness in her chest, she climbs behind the wheel. Her feet barely touch the pedals. The rearview mirror is at an odd angle. The seat is too far reclined.

She sits awkwardly for a moment, thinking of Mike. His presence lingers. Turning the key in the ignition, she adjusts the seat to fit her again. With a sigh, she backs out of the space. Her mind starts to wander as she turns onto the road. Passing the riverside park where they shared their stories, she pictures their first awkward embrace. She remembers their first night in his apartment. Passion that hadn't been in her life since she was a teenager. Since she left him.

She's still sensitive from their last time together; it's hard to believe that it was the last time. It's hard to believe that it happened at all. Now that she's traveling away, it seems more and more like a dream. At the next stop light, she checks her phone for messages.

Disappointment. *What did you think? He's going to text you? Beg you to come back? Get over yourself, girl. With everything you've done to him, you're lucky to have had what you did. He's not coming after you.*

The light turns green. She's moving closer to the interstate. Doubt creeps in. *What am I doing? He's the best thing that ever happened to me. I can't wait to run away from him. What's wrong with me?*

She turns on the radio, hoping music will distract her. *Fucking Bryan Adams. "Please Forgive Me"? God damnit.* "Are you kidding me?" she shouts at the radio. "I fucking hate this song." She doesn't change the station though, and lets the song play.

The lyrics are too much. She's crying in no time. "Fuckin' Bryan Adams." She changes the station. Country. Nope. Next station, hip-hop, something she doesn't recognize. Gah. She pulls up Pandora and plugs it into the radio, puts on her burlesque mix.

I gotta pull myself together. Gotta focus. This is our biggest show ever. Everything will be all right once I'm home. I'll have time for rehearsals. But what am I going to do? How am I going to get up there and be sexy? Pretty sure I used up all my sexy for the week, for the year probably. God. Nothing feels right. It didn't feel right to stay. It doesn't feel right to leave.

Her music plays, so many songs she's performed to, so many that she wants to perform to. But none of them feel right. Dancing doesn't feel right. Nothing feels right. The lights of oncoming traffic shine in the distance. Reflectors and road signs flash on her right. The dotted lines disappear under the van as she drives farther away from him.

***

"Hey there, sleeping beauty." Vic's voice breaks through Mike's restless dreams. "Trouble in paradise already?" Vic drops himself into the chair behind the desk. Mike's folded onto the small couch that sits opposite the desk.

"Not this morning."

His short reply has Vic taken aback. "Sorry, man. I guess I should've known. Can't think of why you would be sleeping on that crappy little couch without reason. What happened?"

Mike sits up, silent, not sure where to begin, or if he even wants to.

"Never mind," Vic mutters. "Forget I asked."

Mike turns his attention to the papers on the desk. "Tell you the truth, I have no idea." He rubs his face, then stretches to release the kink in his back.

"Yeah?" Vic leans back in his chair, his brow knit with curiosity.

Mike slumps into the couch and looks to the ceiling. "Things were going so well. I mean, for the most part. We spent the night at rivercamp."

"Wait. You took her to your hermitage? Shit got real, real fast." He leans forward, elbows on the desk.

"Yeah. I guess they did. Too real. For her anyway. For both of us." Mike brings his hands to his eyes, then pulls them through his hair with a grunt. "I wish I understood that woman. I mean, I was prepared to make it work. You know, her in Chicago, me here. I was ready to drive up there every weekend until one of us couldn't take it anymore.

"I forgave her, damn near begged her to accept my forgiveness. If that makes any sense But she…" His elbows are on his knees, he's staring at the cracks in the floor. "I woke up last night and she was packing her bags to leave. Like she was going to disappear into the night." He looks up.

Vic is listening with his chin resting on his hand. He shakes his head. "That's a real bummer, man. I never saw you care this much if a lady sneaks out in the middle of the night. Pretty sure you actually prefer it that way."

"You got me there. But she's different. I can't explain it." He sits back, his fingers laced in front of his mouth. "When I realized she was leaving, I had to get out. I left her there in the apartment. Walked around, blew off some steam. Then came here to sleep. I'm sure she's gone by now."

Vic nods. "That sucks, man."

"You know the fucked-up part?" Mike leans forward again. "I'm not even mad." He waves one hand in the air. "I'm irritated as all hell, my ego is bruised as fuck, and it hurts like a bitch, but I'm not angry. Don't know what I'm feeling, but it's not anger." He sits there, silent and brooding.

Vic has his laptop out. He's dividing his attention between Mike and whatever business he's tending to. "So, what are you going to do?" Vic glances over the computer and stops typing.

"What do you mean?"

"What do you mean, what do I mean? What are you going to do about her? About yourself? You gonna let her be the one that got away? Again?"

"Fuck you."

"I'm serious, Mike. You've never cared about a woman before. Not that I've seen."

"You make me sound like a prick."

"If the shoe fits."

"Again, fuck you."

"Come on. I've never been a sucker for love myself. But at least I let them down easy."

"Sure." Mike rolls his eyes and sits back again. "I've never had complaints."

"No, you haven't. Only a trail of starry-eyed, love-smitten women who blush every time they see you coming."

"Why are you paying such close attention?" Mike raises an eyebrow.

"Why do you fuck our bar staff?"

"Like you don't."

"Never. Business and pleasure. It makes a mess I don't want to clean up. I've had to do it for you more than once."

"What? Don't be ridiculous."

"I've got one right now who can't work for shit when you're around. You know who I'm talking about. You saw her the other night. Should have seen her face when you left with Amanda."

Mike opens his mouth in defense, remembers the way she looked at him, and closes it. "I've got nothing. I'm a dog. I guess I finally got what's coming to me." He stands and paces the small office space. "What are you doing here so early anyway?"

"Some of us have a business to run."

"Okay. But seven a.m., really?"

"Had to. Left my laptop here and my phone's been going crazy with messages. It might not be the best time to mention it, but people are going crazy for Burlesque A La Mode. We're going to have to book them again. Or another group, I guess. Demand is high."

Mike stops pacing and walks behind Vic, curiosity getting the better of him. "For real?"

Their website wall is full of comments from people who saw the show and loved it, and some who missed it and want to know about the next one. People shared dozens of pictures from the show. Some on and off stage.

And…there she is, caught in a sultry pose, eyes half mast, lips parted. She looks so different from the woman who shared his bed the last few nights, so unreal. But Mike's body reacts, his pulse quickens, his heart breaks. "Goddamn it." He sighs. Vic scrolls to another picture. Mike walks away.

"So, what *are* you going to do?"

"I don't fucking know." He collapses back onto the couch.

Chapter Sixteen

"Bunny." Bridgette is sitting at the tiny table in their kitchen sipping her coffee, her laptop open in front of her.

"Hey, Bridge." Amanda's exhausted, but happy to see her friend. "Everyone asleep?"

"You know they are." Bridgette's hugging Amanda tight. "It's so good to have you back. I missed you. We all did. Want some coffee?" Amanda watches as Bridgette pulls a cup from the cabinet. She pauses. "You look like shit, Bunny. What happened?"

"I don't fucking know." She sits, fighting tears. Bridgette pours the coffee and sits down.

"Wanna talk about it?"

"I don't know." She stares at the coffee in her cup. "I don't know where to begin. I mean there's so much you don't know."

She looks at Bridgette. Her calm eyes and kind smile encourage her to go on.

"You know about my mom and dad, and even Betty. But I never told you about Mike. He was my secret. He was like a fairy tale that I told myself at night when I couldn't sleep. He was the only good thing in my life for a long time, and I left him. I really never thought I would see him again. Was sure that he'd gotten married and had a few kids. I assumed he was living the life we'd dreamed about with someone else in my place. I couldn't believe it when I ran into him, you know?"

Bridgette nods with understanding. Amanda goes on. "He's really amazing." She sniffles. "He does things that you wouldn't believe. He has this way with his voice and his hands…" She grins through tears, shaking her head. "It was so amazing seeing him, being with him." She scoops her sugar and pours her cream. Her gaze falls on Bridgette's. "I don't have words to describe how he made me feel." They sit in silence as Amanda considers what to say next, stirring her coffee.

"So, what are you doing here?" Bridgette asks, tilting her head.

"I'm not sure. He took me home. To the house I lived in with my heartless aunt. I fell apart. He owns her house. She left it to him when she died. It's crazy. She was a harpy. Why would she leave anyone anything?" They both shake their heads.

"I don't know. Maybe she thought it would come back to you someday."

"Not likely. If anything, it was to keep it away from my dad." They sit in silence. "I don't think I can really explain how awful it was being a girl in that house. I'm not sure why I wanted to go back. Mike was there and I was feeling so good. Then he hit me with the fact that he owned the place.

"He never really knew how bad it was. I made sure he didn't. He had been trying to convince me to stay. Maybe he thought if I had a place of my own, I would move right in." Bridgette's calm gaze urges her on. "Maybe I thought I could. But I was wrong. That place was full of ghosts. My childhood was shit. Mike was all I had."

Amanda stares into her coffee cup. No answers there. "No. That's not right. When I was little, it was heaven. Mom and Dad were wonderful. After I was forced to live with my aunt, Mike was the closest thing to that feeling I ever knew."

Her eyes and cheeks are raw from tears. Yet they're rolling down her face again. She wipes at them with her hand, sighs, and goes on. "Then, there's you guys. Who knows where I would be without you. This is the most at home I've felt since I was ten years old. With you guys, here, in my dining/bedroom," she scoffs. "He threw a wrench in all of it. He made me question everything. I guess I couldn't handle it."

"Bunny, you're exhausted. Maybe you should get some sleep. You look like you haven't slept in days."

"I haven't. There's more to it though." She holds her breath, not wanting to say it. "When I moved to Chicago, the first thing I did…" Her voice cracked.

"Maybe you shouldn't."

"No, I have to talk to someone. I took a morning-after pill to terminate a pregnancy. I've never told anyone. I did it all by myself. I'm sure my cousin knew, but she gave me my privacy. We were never close. I was a familial obligation, really. After I took the pill, I had the worst period of my life, followed by months of grief and regret. But I know now, it was the best choice for us. Certainly for him." She sniffled. "And the worst part? He forgave me. He held me and kissed me and took care of me all night after I told him."

She sobbed. Bridgette wrapped her in her arms. "Oh honey, I'm so sorry." She held her tight. "I really think you should lie down."

"I think you're right. Then it's time to get my life back together. Maybe I can get my job back."

"If not that one, then another. Get to sleep. I won't let anyone wake you." They stand, and Bridgette gives her a tight squeeze. "Love you, Bunny. It's good to have you back."

"Love you too."

Through the doorway hung with beads, Amanda passes into her room. The rainbow of tapestries and scarfs greet her along with her humble bed. She drops to the mattress with a sigh, met by squeaky springs.

Kicking off her flip-flops, she climbs under the quilt into cool sheets. Her clothes and costumes hang on a rolling rack in front of her. The morning sun shines through a single lace panel hanging in the window. She closes her eyes.

Exhaustion wins.

She's asleep before her thoughts take over.

**

"Thanks for the lift," Mike says to Vic before getting out of the car at his shop. "It's been a fucked-up week. Best I get back to work."

"That doesn't solve everything, my friend," Vic says before he closes the door.

"It does for now," Mike responds through the open window.

"You know, they're doing a show on Friday night."

"Yeah. I don't think so." He stands up and pats the roof of the car. "See ya."

Inside, he finds Jim and commits himself to the most mind-numbing tasks he can. His frustration must be emanating from him. Everyone avoids him. He's left to work in silence.

Hours pass, and his crew leaves for the day. He's left alone in the empty shop. It seems like years since Amanda shared this space with him, watching as he took her van off the tow truck.

She'd brought life to an otherwise dull place. *Had it really only been four days?* With one job finished and another on deck, he pushes on. Staying busy is all he can do to keep from thinking about her. When there's no more to fix, he turns to cleaning and organizing. Anything to keep him moving.

Day turns to evening, and his stomach growls. He washes up and heads to the office, where a stack of invoices waits for him. And memories. Her flushed cheeks as he tweaked her nipples and whispered in her ear. The bashful way she exposed herself to him. Her shock and frustration when she realized what kind of game they were playing.

He smiles despite the pain in his chest.

At his desk, he sorts through the pile of paperwork, then turns to his computer. Temptation gets the better of him, and he's searching for pictures of Bunny Demure.

She's everywhere. She's on stage, and in various locations. So many photos, by several photographers, one in particular, O'Hare. That familiar pain in his chest returns at the sight of the shot that he had loved so much where she's bare and natural, exactly the way he loves her.

Obviously the way someone else had too. *Is this who she had to hurry back to?* It didn't matter who O'Hare was. She was gone.

Amanda had chosen the life she'd had over life with him, and that was the end of it.

He shuts down the computer with disgust and leans back in his chair, unsure of where to go from here.

***

"Bunny." She can smell Calvin's cologne before her eyes are open. His arms are around her, his cheek against hers. "So glad you're home." He squeezes, tight. Another body hits the bed. The springs protest with a squeak.

"Welcome home, girl." Jessica crawls up beside her, wrapping both her and Calvin in her arms. Amanda is smiling through sleepy eyes at her friends as they hold her close. Jonathan joins them, sitting at her feet, eating a banana.

"We were sure we'd lost you," Jonathan teases.

"What time is it?" she asks.

"Just after four," Calvin answers. "You gonna sleep 'til Friday?"

"From the looks of it, she might need to," Jonathan chimes in, his mouth full.

"I missed you guys. Except you," she sneers and kicks at Jonathan, missing intentionally.

"Oh, come on, Bunny. I bet you missed me most of all." He laughs.

"I feel like Dorothy waking up from her adventure in Oz. And you were there, and you were there, and you…" She sits up, looking from one beautiful face to another. "But I think there are too many people in this bed right now. Besides, I was only gone for a few days. I know for a fact Cindy has shacked up elsewhere for much longer on more than one occasion."

"True. But we like you more." Jonathan chuckles and slaps her knee. "But, really, you never leave. You're like a houseplant." He stands up and laughs again.

"You're a houseplant," she mutters after him. The joy of seeing her friends is slowly ebbing. *He's right,* she thinks. *I am a houseplant. A houseplant that made the worst mistake of her life.* She closes her eyes again and sees Mike's face.

"You're our favorite houseplant, though. I mean, you water yourself and everything."

"Go away, Jonathan."

"You cut me deep, Bunny. Real deep," he says, holding his hand to his heart, leaving the room.

"Spill it, girl," Calvin says, patting her shoulder. "Let's hear about your week with that delicious mountain of a man."

"I don't even know where to begin. But it doesn't matter much anyway. I'm never seeing him again."

"What happened?" Jessica asks, sitting up.

"I don't really want to talk about it," Amanda says, kicking her blankets off and standing up. "I need to figure out what I can do about getting my job back."

Jessica and Calvin share curious looks behind her as she inspects her weary face in the mirror above her dresser. "I'm not convincing anyone to give me anything with this face," she says to their reflection in her mirror.

"You sure you don't want to talk about it?" Jessica asks, standing and approaching her from behind. They look at each other in the mirror.

"I messed up. That's all." She shudders and shakes it away. Jessica looks at her with pity in her eyes.

"If you want to talk, I'm here." Jessica hugs her from behind.

"I know," Amanda says, patting her hand on Jessica's waist. "Thanks."

"Wanna go get some food?"

"I'm starving," Calvin whines from the bed and jumps up, patting his belly.

"You guys go. I'll get something later."

Jessica squeezes her tight. She and Calvin leave. Amanda's left staring at her reflection, alone again. Her old friend numbness returns. She looks at her phone. No messages. Her heart sinks. *What did you think? He's not going to try to reach you. You made your wishes clear.*

Did I though?

The whole night before she left was such a confusing, emotional disaster. She isn't even sure what was said anymore. She does remember the way he left her, holding tight to his anger and his heartbreak.

Maybe I should send him a message, let him know I'm home safe.

She holds her phone in her hand, wishing she had taken a picture of him, but she didn't need one. She saw him every time she closed her eyes.

Home safe

She stares at the screen, unable to hit send.

***

This bartender is too good at her job, he thinks as she brings him another beer. She's older than him, but not old. Her eyes tell a story of a life full of nights like this. Stuck in a dive bar, serving drunks and brokenhearted fools. What Mike wouldn't give to be one of the former. She winks and walks away, knowing when to make pleasantries and when to make herself scarce. He watches her unnaturally fluffy, bleach-blonde hair and wonders if it feels like cotton candy, if it's ever been pulled the right way. Then he remembers Amanda's silken tresses wrapped around his fingers. His time with her becomes a series of snapshots. A tilted smile, a rosy nipple, the curve of her hip, her legs, her hair, her lips, kisses, nibbles, giggles.

"Gah." He shrugs and finds the bottom of the bottle.

A glance to the bartender and she's back again, open bottle in hand. "Thanks," he grunts, taking the beer. Looking to the bottles on the back of the bar, he considers ordering a shot or five, anything to make going home to an empty apartment easier. He swallows half the bottle in one gulp. It's good and cold and going down easy. He finishes and sets it on the bar.

"You didn't drive here, did you?" the bartender asks as she brings another open bottle. Mike shakes his head in response and takes the offered bottle.

"Thanks." He nods and takes another drink, smaller than the last two. Though he can feel his head swimming.

"Good." She seems to be testing the waters of conversation. The gleam in her eye tells Mike she'd like to flirt. Maybe even take him home. For a moment he considers the possibilities. *Maybe she could teach me a thing or two.* He smiles and drinks some more, looking her over, from her frizzy hair to her faded eyes, the wrinkles around her mouth and the papery brown skin of her cleavage. She's nothing compared to what he held in his arms the night before.

"I'll close my tab," he says, nodding to his bottle before he takes another drink.

"All right," she says with a smile and a hint of disappointment.

Outside, Mike stands on the sidewalk, not completely sure of which direction he's headed. Judging from his tab and the wavy world around him, he'd had a few more than he'd intended.

Letting his feet make the call, aimlessly, he strolls along the familiar streets. Past clubs and restaurants, people smoking and carrying on. He walks, blurry eyes, numb mind. Bar signs flash and strings of lights twinkle in the trees. He keeps moving and turns the corner. His feet carry him away from the noise.

Before he knows it, he's at the river, elbows on the cast-iron rail. The black water ripples along. The big white moon shimmers on the surface. His liquid dinner has done the trick. Head buzzing, he watches the water. Then Amanda is there in the periphery of his mind, laughing and sharing her story. He recalls the moment their lips came together. It had been like nothing he could recall. Not even the first time so many years before could compare. Pure elation, his cells recognized her in an instant.

"Fuck," he grumbles, standing upright. Pulling his phone from his pocket, he checks his messages. Nothing.

His head swims; he's thirsty. He heads home to an empty apartment.

***

"He's an asshole anyway, Bunny," Cindy says. "Tell you the truth, I'm looking for a new job too." They're watching Lucy as she moves through her routine for the next night. The theater gave them one night for dress rehearsal. Jonathan was in the sound booth with their light and sound guy, going over cues.

"What happens if we all stop working there though? Do we lose our connection? Should we start looking for another venue?" Amanda asks.

"Are you kiddin' me? You know how much money we make that dickhole? Besides, look around," she says, her eyes bright. "We're moving up. After tomorrow night, we won't need that place anymore. We'll be here."

"Let's hope. But now I have to find a new job. I hate looking."

"No one likes looking for work. We're lucky though People like to hire pretty girls to tend bar."

"True. What are you doing for the show tomorrow? I'm so out of the loop, I feel like I've been gone for months instead of days."

"Something new. I'm tired of everything I've been doing. How about you?"

"God, I'm not sure. I don't feel it right now. The idea of getting up there and seducing a room full of strangers." She looks away from her friend to the now-empty stage. "I don't know what to do."

"What the hell did that man do to you? I've never seen you like this." Cindy smacks her shoulder.

"I don't even know where to begin." She's looking at her hands, remembering how his body felt under them. Then she looks at her friend. "I love him, Cin. So much. And I fucked up again." Her voice cracks. Cindy pulls her into a big, tight hug.

"It's all right, girl. Everything will work out in the end. You know what I always say. You have to take this vulnerability and put it on the stage." She pats her back and pulls away, her hands still on Amanda's shoulders. "I know you have it in you. I knew the day I met you that you had glitter in your veins. You're beautiful up there. People are always spellbound. You do something from the heart and there won't be a dry eye in the joint. Maybe dickhead will feel bad enough to give you your job back," she says with a smile and nod toward the bar.

"Doubtful. But thanks. I think I know what to do. Remember the one I did in the blue dress last year for that one event?"

Cindy stares at her with her mouth agape, one eyebrow raised. "Sure I do. It was the night I danced to that one song in that one pair of heels." Her voice is laced with sarcasm.

"You'll remember. It was off the cuff, some last-minute stuff."

"You need some stage time?"

"Nah, I have to listen to the song though. You want vulnerable, I can't practice that."

"You should go talk to light and sound though, give 'em something to work with."

Chapter Seventeen

The hours creep by when you're heartbroken and hungover. Mike is learning the lesson firsthand. The sound of power tools makes his headache worse. The smell of everyone's lunch turns his stomach. He sits at his desk, staring at a pile of paperwork he couldn't care less about. His phone sits beside the stack. Aside from an unanswered message from Vic, it's been dead all day. His mouth tastes like a swamp and feels like a desert. He drops his heavy head onto the desk.

Jim comes through the door asking a question that Mike doesn't hear. "You all right, boss?"

Mike sits up. "What? Fuck." He looks up. "Long night."

"I can tell. You look like shit, man."

"Feel worse. I'm leaving. Gotta go sleep this off. You got this?"

"Sure thing."

"Thanks." Mike stands, grabs his phone, and heads out the door, bell ringing behind him. The sun and heat are enough to make a man want to crawl under a rock and die. He chooses a better option. In his truck and headed to the cabin, his head and stomach are doing a bit better. Stopping once for water and food, his spirits are lifted as the city falls behind and the country spreads out around him.

His phone buzzes. It's Vic.

-How's it going?-

-Heading out to the cabin. I'll stop in when I get back-

He drops the phone beside him on the bench seat. It buzzes back. He ignores it, letting the wind through the window be his only companion.

A long nap and some night fishing will help with this hangover. Focusing on the road ahead, he looks forward to his big soft bed. He'll drink his weight in water and sleep the day away. *Things will look better tonight. I've gotten over her once before. I can do it again.*

He pulls up at the cabin. The bird song welcomes him as he steps down from the truck. It puts him at ease. With water and food in hand he heads into the cabin. He chugs a bottle as he checks his phone, from Vic.

-Enjoy the hermitage-

He leaves the phone on the counter and turns to the bed. Pushing Amanda out of his mind, he collapses onto it and pulls a pillow over his pounding head. The world disappears. Hours pass, afternoon into evening. He wakes up, drinks more water, and lies back down. The pounding has subsided into a dull ache. He considers fishing but decides against it. The dreamless sleep of exhaustion is the only thing he's up for. It is, however, not what he gets.

Her arms are there wrapping around his neck. She's slid into his bed. Then it's her lips pressed to his, on his face, his chest. Her teeth bite down on his chin. Her hands run over the length of his body everywhere, all at once. His eyes are closed, he sees nothing. But she's there. Her presence is thick in the air, a giggle, a coo, a sigh. Then nothing.

And he's smothered. Choking on her absence. He wakes in a pool of sweat alone. Only the light from the moon greets him, glinting off something in the darkness. He flips on the bedside lamp. On the couch lies her collar. The heart-shaped tag shines. He reaches for it. The tag reads on one side "Hunny Bunny." On the other one word: "Yours."

His heart drops out of his chest.

One word is all it takes.

He lies back with one realization. He's made the greatest mistake of his life for the second time.

She's always been his.

All he ever had to do was prove that he wanted all of her, every broken piece. He should have chased her down so many years ago, when she ran away crying. If he would have let go of his injured pride and followed her, if he had begged her to stay, told her what she meant to him, what losing her felt like, he knows now, she would have stayed.

They could have had their whole life. Instead, they lost years, and so much more. And what did he do with the second chance he was given? He let his pride win again. He shut down and ran away. Surely, she would have stayed the second time. If he would have sat beside her and had shown her his heart, every crack with her name on it, every memory that he held so dear. All he had to do was prove that he was as much hers as she was his.

He searches for his phone and checks the time. Just after eleven. With the collar in one hand he types a message to Vic with the other.

-You down for a trip to Chicago?-

The weight in his chest is gone. He feels lighter with every step. Mindlessly, he eats one of the extra sandwiches he brought while he finds the venue she's performing in and books his room nearby.

He thinks of sending her a message, but resists. He wants to see her in her element, without his influence, wants to see her performing like she was the first time he saw her on stage. His phone buzzes.

-Fuck yeah. I'm down.-

-Good deal. I'm leaving late tomorrow morning. Got some shit to take care of at work. I'll meet you at the club.-

-I'll be there-

***

"Who's got bobby pins?" Amanda shouts over the clamor of the dressing room. "My hair will not stay in place."

"It would if you'd stop touching it," Cindy, in a wig cap and half her makeup, shouts back from the other side of the room.

"I don't know, Cin. It keeps falling flat. I'm trying to make it right." Cindy crosses to her and smacks her hand away.

"We go through this every time. Leave the curls alone. They'll stay if you let them." She's looking up at Amanda, fluffing and teasing her hair into place. "Besides, you look best in that messy, just-got-fucked hair anyway." She pauses. "But that's not the look you're going for is it?"

"Not really. Have you seen the dress I'm wearing?" She motions to the costume rack in the corner. Blue sequins spill out of her open garment bag. Cin narrows her eyes.

"Sit down. I'll pin you up even though I know it'll be down before the night is over." She shakes her head and pins Amanda's hair up with effortless skill.

"Thank you." Amanda smiles her most grateful smile, batting her eyes.

"Your makeup is on point tonight," Cindy states, assessing her look. "You're getting good at this shit."

"Thanks to you." She looks at Cindy's unfinished makeup and asks, "Are you good? Do you need anything?"

"Gotta finish painting my face and put my hair on. I'm not on 'til later anyway." Cindy turns away. "Anyone else need anything?" she hollers over the room. The room responds with various noes or head shakes. "Then I'm gonna smoke." She pulls on a silk robe and heads for the back door. "Anyone coming with?" Lucy and Calvin jump up to follow. The rest go back to their mirrors.

Amanda sits in silence, watching as everyone fusses with their faces and hair. It feels like home, but empty at the same time. Suddenly, the allure of the stage is a lot less alluring.

Bridgette sits down beside her. "You all right?" she asks, her hand on Amanda's knee.

"Yeah. I think so." Amanda looks into her friend's eyes. They are full of understanding. "I can't stop thinking about him." She blinks back tears, her false lashes fluttering.

"Don't cry, Bunny. You'll ruin your makeup." Bridgette calms her, dabbing at the corners of her eyes with a tissue. "In a couple hours we can veg out with some ice cream and tears. But for now, you've got to pull it together."

"I know." She takes a deep breath and blows it out, reaching for a piece of hair that's fallen loose.

"Don't touch." Cindy's hand comes down from behind her, smacking her hand away.

"Ouch. I swear, you look forward to doing that. That one hurt too." Amanda holds her injured hand with an insolent pout.

"And I swear, you fuck with your hair just to make me angry."

"It's not my fault. My hair has a mind of its own."

"And so do your hands. Gregor is here tonight. No pressure. I thought you might want a heads-up. You know you're his favorite."

"Are you kidding? I'm sure he's got a camera at every angle and one around his neck. I certainly hope I don't disappoint." She sighs and stands, adjusting her robe. "Also, I'm not his favorite. He's here to film us all. Burlesque is his true love."

"I always wondered why you never gave him a chance. I know I'd let him take me out a time or two," Cindy teases. "But now that I've met your superman…"

"Not now, Cin. I can't think of him right now. What time is it?" Amanda asks.

"It's almost showtime, Bunny," Jonathan answers as he enters the room. "You ready?"

"Almost."

"All right. We got Malcolm and Sarah's duet. Then Lucy. Then Bunny." He's counting with one hand and pointing with the other. "Are you two ready?" He nods toward Jessica and Calvin. They're dancing in a corner.

"Yep," Jessica responds, chipper and confident.

"Always," Calvin says with his silky smooth voice.

"How 'bout you, Lucy?"

"I will be."

"Well, let's do this then." Jonathan disappears through the door.

Amanda stands in front of a full-length mirror. Her robe hangs open, revealing her sparkling blue pasties and sequin-covered thong. Her skin is dusted with silver glitter. After so many years, she still doesn't recognize the woman staring back at her. The wonders of makeup and attitude.

Turning toward the garment rack, she reaches for the corset first. It's covered in sequins and is sky blue. *The color of his eyes.* She shakes her head with a scoff. The satin lining slides around her waist. She sets each clasp in place from the bottom to the top. It hugs her tight. Pulling at the lace in the back, she watches as her waist shrinks in the mirror.

The hair, makeup, and corset all come together. Stepping into the sea of sparkling blue that is her gown, she pulls it up and zips it into place. She's transformed. There is no room for her broken heart behind the satin and sequins. Each silver shoe slides on like Cinderella's glass slippers. She holds her satin gloves in one hand, waiting to put them on.

Around the room, she sees her friends transformed as well. They spend most of their time in sweats and loungewear. To see them all lit up with stage faces and beautiful costumes is always a sight.

"Everyone looks amazing," she says, still holding her gloves.

Jessica and Calvin are standing by the stage door. Jessica in a skintight galaxy dress. Calvin, with the same print on his pants and tie. Gold and silver glitter sparkle on their cheeks and shoulders. Lucy's in black from head to toe. The flaming red of her hair the only color she wears. Her oversize headdress of flowers and chains is fierce. Even her lips are black. They spread into a huge smile as she laughs at something someone said.

The juxtaposition of her look and her laugh aren't lost on Amanda. "Except you, Lucy. You are a walking lie." She squints her eyes and snarls in mock disgust.

"Well, you look like a whore. A cheap, filthy whore."

"I may look like a whore, but at least I look good. You on the other hand…" She gags. "You make me want to barf in my mouth." Lucy shakes her head. Neither one is sure where their feigned rivalry began. However, it has become a comforting ritual for them both.

"I hate your face."

"I hate your hair."

"I hate you." They laugh together, pulling each other into an embrace.

"You're going to kill it."

"So are you."

Calvin and Jessica disappear through the door. Jonathan appears in their place. "Another great crowd. They're rowdy tonight."

"That's how we like 'em," Cindy says from her mirror. They can hear the cheers coming from the crowd and the bass from Calvin and Jessica's music. "Sounds like they missed us."

Amanda paces. Calvin and Jessica come back, grinning and out of breath. Jonathan exits. The crowd gives another big round of applause. Lucy is waiting for her cue.

"You aren't nervous, are you?" Lucy asks, her head tilted.

"No," Amanda answers with a laugh. "I can't sit in this thing. It snags on everything." What she's feeling is so much worse than nerves. Regret and heartbreak play their rhythm in her soul.

Lucy exits to the sound of more applause.

Jonathan enters. "You look great, Bunny. Ready?"

"Yep." The moments waiting to go on are the longest.

Lucy pushes through the door, next to naked in a thong and pasties. She's panting and smiling.

Amanda checks her reflection one more time and takes her place by the door. With her eyes closed she waits to hear her name, rubbing her satin-gloved hands together. She channels her most sultry self and embraces the vulnerability.

Jonathan pushes through the door, holding it open for her. The sound of applause lures her on.

Beth Rowley's haunting voice sings "Nobody's Fault But Mine." The music is soft and soulful. Amanda steps onto the dimly lit stage. The lights come up, hitting every sequin. Thunderous applause greets her.

She sparkles with each slow, intentional step, swept away by the energy in the room. The lyrics, however, bring her back to her vulnerability. She pulls at one glove, heart aching. Then the other. The chorus rings again. Tears form in her eyes; she blinks them away.

The crowd is silent. She spins and pulls at her zipper, sure that she's lost them. But as she peels away the gown, they erupt again. She turns back to them to reveal her corseted waist and free, bouncing, pasty-covered breasts. They are cheering wildly with hoots and whistles.

At a moment when she should be elated, she's numb. The tears flow freely as she gives up holding down the lump in her throat. She hurries off the stage. Passing Jonathan, and pushing through the bodies waiting to go on, she heads straight for the bathroom.

"Bunny?" Bridgette is knocking softly.

"I'm fine. I need a minute," she squeaks through stifled sobs. Her reflection tells another story. Mascara and eyeliner run down her face, streaking her perfectly contoured cheeks. Her red eyes ache. She shudders. Moments pass as her black tears fall into the sink.

"Bunny?" Calvin calls, knocking again. "Clean up that face, girl. I've got something for you."

Puzzled, she opens the door.

Chapter Eighteen

Jonathan introduces her. "Ladies and gentlemen, Bunny Demure."

Mike cheers along with the energetic crowd. She steps out onto the dark stage. The lights come up. Applause explodes as every inch of her seems to sparkle and gleam. He's spellbound as she moves slowly across the stage.

Her eyes are down. He knows the look all too well. Her heart is broken. She's fighting tears. He doesn't recognize the music she moves to. But the sadness and longing are familiar. One silver glove slips off her hand. The crowd hoots and hollers.

She rewards them with a smile that shines brighter than every sequin on her dress. She turns away with a wiggle, dabbing at her eye with the glove in her hand. *Does everyone see this? She's crying up there.*

The applause dies down. She turns back with a forced smile and pulls at the second glove with slow precision. She's unreal. Beautiful, yet so different from the woman his heart knows. The lips he dreamed of kissing are painted deep red and glossy. Her eyes, framed with false lashes and glitter, can't hide the regret.

Is she up there wishing she were with me? That she hadn't left?

He notices the quiet in the room and realizes she's fooling no one. As beautiful as she is to look at, the room at large struggles with the desire to see more, and the guilt that comes along with watching a woman dance with tears in her eyes.

He also notices a handsome man in a suit holding a camera to his eye, right off the front of the stage. He's snapping pictures wildly. She blinks. Her eyes dazzle again. With a twirl and a sigh, she's won them back. Unzipping her zipper, she peels away her gown and steps out of the glimmering blue that pools at her feet.

Is that fucking O'Hare? I knew it. They were probably fighting before she went on stage. That explains the tears.

The crowd is cheering again. Her waist is tiny in the shimmering corset. Her full breasts rise and fall as she spins to the audience, revealing her pasty-covered finale. The photographer down front is still snapping away. *This was a huge mistake.* Mike is ready to find Vic and slip out unnoticed. One more glance to the stage. Her smile is gone, she sighs again, her shoulders slump. Tears are running freely, streaking her flushed cheeks with black. She turns and hurries off the stage.

Don't be a fool. You came all this way. Mike's heart is beating out of his chest. He scans the room, looking for the backstage entrance. He sees the photographer moving toward a door on the wall. He pushes through the group between him and the same door.

Jonathan has returned to stage. Everyone is cheering for the brokenhearted Bunny Demure. Mike finds a door behind the curtain and knocks. No response. He steps back and looks for an exit sign or anything telling him he's on the right track. O'Hare, or whatever his name is, steps between him and the door.

"Can I help you?" he asks, looking up.

Mike's first instinct is to push him to the side and continue knocking at the door. Whoever he is, this guy has confirmed that he is in the right place. Vic appears at his side.

"I think my friend was looking for the bathroom," Vic says with all the charm and cunning he possesses.

Mike looks from the photographer to the door behind him. "No. I'm looking for backstage." He grinds his teeth, glaring at O'Hare. *This guy and that door are all that are holding me back. I could easily take them both.*

His hands are clenched in fists at his side. He takes a deep breath and opens his mouth to tell the photographer exactly what he can do to help. The door opens behind him. Calvin's face pokes out. The look of recognition on his face saves the day. He steps out, holding his silky robe closed at the chest.

"He's okay, *Greg.* He's here to see Bunny," Calvin says, placing his hand on the photographer's shoulder. "He's late. Should have been here sooner." He winks at Mike.

"You sure?" Greg looks from Calvin to Mike, puffing his chest out with laughable posturing. Then, realizing he's been bested.

"Yes, I'm sure. How could I mistake a tall drink of water like this?" Calvin stands almost as tall as Mike and looks down at Greg as well. Between the two of them and Vic, O'Hare admits defeat and slinks away.

"Thanks," Mike says as Calvin pushes the door open and ushers them in.

"He hates when I call him that." Calvin laughs.

"What's he like to be called?" Mike asks, still curious about him.

"Gregor," Calvin exclaims, waving his hands in the air. "Gregor Hart," he says with a poor British accent and laughs to himself.

"Not O'Hare?"

More laughter. "No. That's O'Hare." Calvin points at the small blonde stretching with her hula hoop.

"That's O'Hare?"

"Yeah. Is that who you came to see? Thought you were here for Bunny." Calvin's voice drips with attitude.

"Sorry, I was confused. Yes, Bun- Amanda."

"She's in the bathroom."

Mike stands in the doorway, Vic at his side. They look around, surveying the disaster that is the dressing room. Clothes are draped on nearly every piece of furniture. Bags lie open, spilling their contents on the ground. Makeup cases and mirrors are set up on any free space of wall.

Women stand in various stages of undress. Some with pasties, some completely bare. It's any schoolboy's fantasy come true. Calvin tiptoes through the maze and knocks at the door opposite Mike, saying something low into the door.

Amanda opens the door, the definition of a hot mess. "What?" she asks, as Calvin steps aside. Her gaze lands on Mike, wide with shock.

Her mouth hangs open, speechless.

***

Mike is standing across the room, mere steps away. Their gazes meet. He smiles. Amanda runs across the room to his open arms. Crushed to his chest, she's shaking with joy.

He's here. He's right here. How did I ever think I could live without him again?

With her hands on his chest, she looks into his face. He's beaming down at her. On her toes, she nuzzles his bristly chin. His lips press against her forehead.

"What are you doing here?" she asks, barely a whisper.

"Isn't it obvious?" He raises an eyebrow and loosens his hold. She settles onto her feet. His hands rest on her hips as they stand together, studying each other. Crinkles streak out of his eyes with his grin. "I came for the show." He's looking her over. She looks down.

"Oh god. I'm a disaster." She steps back, away from him. "Give me a minute." Turning to run to the bathroom, she sees most of her friends. They're watching the scene, clearly moved by the reunion.

Bridgette smiles from the stage door, waiting for her cue to go on. She's blotting at her eyes.

"Dammit, Bunny."

Amanda sniffles and giggles as she hurries past them all.

***

He's standing with Vic at his side. Every sparkling eye is on them. Cindy is completely nude with a can of spray adhesive in one hand and something that resembles a jockstrap in the other. Calvin leans against the wall beside the bathroom door, his hand over his heart with a silly grin. Mike doesn't remember all their names. But he can almost see the big hearts and bluebirds dancing around their heads.

"I think," he pauses, "we'll wait out there. Catch the rest of the show."

"Ladies." Vic nods to them all as they make their exit.

Back in the lowlights of the bar, they find a new place near the stage door where they can still see the show. Greg gives them the evil eye from across the room. Mike brushes it off. Nothing can bring him down. The love of his life is on the other side of that door. She'll be in his arms in moments and he'll never let her go again.

"I booked two rooms for us," he says under his breath as they watch Baby hula hoop her way around the stage. The shouts and whistles of the audience drown out the music. How she does it while taking her clothes off is nothing short of amazing.

"I assumed no less," Vic responds, his eyes fixed on Baby.

"As soon as she comes through that door, I'm leaving."

"I think I'll manage." Vic smiles, clearly plotting schemes about who he's going to get back in his room tonight. With a quick glance Mike's way, he adds, "At the very least, I'll get to see the rest of the show. These girls are good."

"Yeah." Mike's nervous, watching the door. It all happened so quickly before. She was in his arms before he could consider the consequences. After that, it was one thrilling embrace after another, until she left. Now, he's had hours to contemplate, consider, and reflect. He's had hours to think of everything that could go wrong, every word he could stumble over, every mistake he could make, and all the hours without her.

The pain of her absence is so fresh.

Whatever happens, I'm not giving up this time.

***

"Did any of you know about this?" Amanda shouts from the bathroom, suds foaming on her face as she washes the makeup away.

"Nope." Calvin leans on the doorframe. "But I wish I had. That was the sweetest thing I've ever seen." He steps behind her to admire his reflection.

She smiles at him. "I don't have words for how I'm feeling right now." Their gazes meet in the mirror. Then, she bends to the sink to wash the soap away.

"Whatever it is, it looks good on you." She grins as she dries her face with a hand towel. Pulling at the pins Cindy placed earlier, she watches her hair tumble down. She runs her fingers through it, pulling the curls loose, and then leaves Calvin with his reflection.

"I knew it," Cindy yells with a playful tug on Amanda's hair.

"I'm sorry. I had to." She stops in front of Cindy, who's pulling the second layer of her costume over her hips.

"It's all right. Good to see you smiling again."

"It feels good. I can't believe he's here." Looking around for her bag. "I don't think I'll make it to curtain call."

"I wouldn't either if I had that one waiting for me." She nods toward the door. Amanda giggles, reaching back to loosen her corset. Her ribs relax as her lungs fill with their first full breath of air.

She braces herself for what comes next. With a sigh and a yank, the pasties come free from her nipples. Losing the sequin-covered panties, she bends for her bag and starts packing her things. Donning a comfortable sundress from the garment rack, she checks the room for anything else.

"Sorry, I'm leaving you guys with the mess."

"We'll get it."

"Love you all." She grabs her bag again and heads for the door.

The numb, empty feeling is gone. It's been replaced with sweaty palms and heart palpitations, and a fluttering zeal that she's never known.

**

The show proceeds, and as entertaining as it is, Mike shifts uncomfortably against the wall. His thoughts are on the evening ahead.

For many in the room this is the highlight of their night, their week even. For him, it's a precursor. The joy of holding her again, of seeing the undeniable love in her eyes, was inconceivable.

The door opens. She's standing in a sundress, her hair down, her face lit with a smile only for him. He hurries to her side, taking her bag in one hand. The other he places on the small of her back.

"Can we get out of here?" he asks, leaning close to her ear to be heard over the music and clamor of the crowd.

"Yes." She leads him to the back exit.

"My hotel isn't far from here."

"Good."

The sound of her voice stirs something only she can.

On the street, a hot wind blows around them both as they pass by throngs of people. Amanda's hair and dress come to life with each heavy gust. She laughs, trying to tame them both.

"I'm sorry," she says as they walk.

"Don't be," he responds, wanting to keep the good feelings rolling.

"No. I am. I shouldn't have run."

"I shouldn't have pushed you."

"You didn't push."

"I did. I feel like I did everything wrong. I should have let you take your time. Should have been happy with what we had."

"We both fucked up," she says. "I knew the minute you left your place that I made a huge mistake." They walk in silence.

"That's what I'm saying. I shouldn't have left you."

"I'm the one who left."

"But I didn't try to stop you."

"I don't think you would have been able to."

"No?" He stops, she does the same. People pass on either side like water in a stream. He's looking down, into her face. She's smiling up at him.

"I'm a stubborn fool."

"Stubborn, yes. Fool? Ehhh…" he teases.

"Yes." She nods. "How could I run away from you twice? I've never been happier than when I'm with you."

"I know the feeling."

"Do you?"

"I'm here, aren't I?"

She smiles again, happy tears glittering in her eyes. "You are." She places her hand on his chest and bites her lower lip. "Now what?"

"Now, we keep moving. I want you all to myself."

"Yes," she agrees. They start walking again, their steps longer, pace quicker.

***

She stands in the middle of his suite, a large mirror in front of her, a king-size bed behind. Mike stands at the door, securing the bolt. He places her bag on the floor and steps toward her.

"You were beautiful up there tonight," he says, closing the distance between them. "But I don't think you've ever looked more beautiful than you do right now."

He lifts her hair off her shoulders with both hands, sweeping it back. His hands linger on her shoulders. Heat spreads from where they touch her skin to her sex. His eyes search hers. She holds his gaze with the same intensity.

"Because you're here, with me. There's only one thing…" He trails off, his eyes glancing to her dress. Sliding his thumbs into the straps, he slips them off her shoulders. The dress is loose fitting. It falls to the ground, a thrilling whisper down her body. She's pulsing with joy as he admires her newly naked form. "That's better."

"Almost," she responds, reaching for the buttons of his shirt. His hand closes over hers.

"Wait." Puzzled, she looks up. "Walk for me, over there." He motions to the window.

"Okay," she says, pulling her hand from his. She turns and steps away from him, her eyes on the wall ahead. With slow, measured steps she comes to the wall and turns back to him. Raising her hands with a performer's flair, she smiles. He sits on the foot of the bed, eyes still on her. "Now what?"

"Come back to me." His voice is low, not the saccharine sweet tone he's used in the past. It's soft, timid even. She crosses the room and kneels between his legs, placing her hands on either knee. He rests his on top of hers.

"Tell me that's the last time you'll walk away." His voice catches in his throat. "Tell me you're done running." He squeezes her hand gently. She looks in his eyes. There's a sadness in them she knows all too well. "Because..." He clears his throat, looks away. "As lovely a sight as it is to watch you go," he scoffs at himself, "I never want to see it again."

Shaking his head, he looks back at her, with a tight smile. She slides her hands out from under his and stands up on her knees, bringing her forehead to his. With her hands in the coarse hair of his beard, she kisses his mouth.

"I'm done running," she says, eyes closed. Her voice is soft, but her words have never been more sure.

She opens her eyes to his. They're full of longing, desire, an ache she wants to kiss away. "I'll never walk away from you again."

She kisses his face, his forehead, his brow. His arms slide around her back, pulling her closer to him. Their lips meet. She sighs into the kiss, running her hands down his neck, to the soft hair on his chest.

One clumsy button after another, she reveals the warmth of his bare skin. She presses her cool breasts to him. *Home.* Wherever she is, if this man is there, she'll know she belongs.

Climbing onto his legs, she straddles him while pulling his shirt off. As her arms encircle his back, she's overwhelmed. His heat rivals the very sun. She presses herself even closer, wanting to feel every inch of his skin against hers.

His arms answer the call. They are wrapped in one another's embrace, his face between her breasts, her cheek against the top of his head. His hands run over her back, up and down. He kisses her breasts, her chest, her neck. She holds tighter still, then pushes him back. Sliding off his knees to the floor, she sits on her feet and pulls at the buckle of his belt. With some help he's sitting before her as naked as she is, cock solid and waiting.

She aches for it. Taking it in her mouth, she sucks at the tip, holding it there, exploring with her tongue. He falls back on the bed with a moan. Stroking and suckling, she rocks on her knees. His hips answer every pull.

Sitting up, he holds her face. She stops and looks up. He guides her onto the bed, laying her down. His hand travels over her body, caressing every slope and curve.

She rolls with joy as one hand runs over her nipples and the other slips two fingers into her dripping sex. He's kneeling beside her, the picture of masculinity. Then, he's above her, spreading her legs with his knees. He holds himself up with one arm while the other rubs his thick, swollen head over her clit.

Heart pounding, she arches her body against his. Sliding the tip in, he circles the opening. She cries out, "Oh, please more." He answers with every inch.

She's screaming and panting with each thrust and digging her nails into his shoulders. He stops and rolls her onto her stomach, pulling her hips to meet him. He's slow at first, fingers caressing her hip bones. Then, without warning he grips her hard, pounding frantically.

As soon as she succumbs to the force, he slows his pace. Leaning down, he nuzzles her neck, pinching one nipple. Then, biting her shoulder, he returns to his wild pace. Face buried in the blankets, her hips rise to meet him. He pulls out and clutches her hips, dragging her across the bed. She rolls onto her back. "I wanna ride you."

"By all means." He lies down.

"Mmmm." She climbs over him, sliding down onto his shaft. The fullness is exquisite as she takes him in. His hands roam her body, leaving tendrils of ecstasy. With her hands on the solid mass of his chest, she digs her nails in. Rocking with abandon, waves of delight course through her. He's gripping and lifting her hips, pushing deeper still, until he joins her in rapture.

They roll together onto their sides, still entangled with one another.

***

"I'm glad I'm here," he says. He's holding her beside him. They're sitting up against the pillows on the wall. Her head rests on his chest.

"Me too," she breathes. "I don't know what I was thinking."

"It doesn't matter now," he says with a shoulder squeeze. "I believe you said it yourself. This can work. A little patience goes a long way."

"I don't want to be patient. I want to be with you," she says, sitting up. Her eyes are on his. "Two nights without you were awful enough. I don't want to do it again. I know I'll miss these guys, but nowhere near as much as I've missed you."

"Good to hear, but you'll still be seeing them regularly, I'd wager."

"What do you mean?"

"What would you say to a full-time gig at the Speakeasy? Vic and I were talking on the way here. We've had an excellent response from your show last week. We think there's a market for regular shows. You can bring these guys in or start your own troupe with local girls. Or both."

She's smiling at him, her mind on the future. "Are you serious?"

"Yep. What do you think?"

"Oh my god. Mike. I don't know what to say."

"Say you'll come home with me."

"How could I not?" she squeals and throws her arms around his neck. "I love you so much. I don't know how you could make me happier than I am right now."

"Challenge accepted," he says and wraps her in his arms.

Next in the Burlesque River series is Bridgette's story:
Burlesque on Bourbon.

ABOUT THE AUTHOR

Kitty Bardot juggles a life full of excitement and love. By day, she's a chef with her own catering company, by night she puts tens years of burlesque experience to use in various venues in the Quad Cities. She writes from her country home not far from the Mississippi River, enjoying every moment with her husband and their three children. Currently, she is working on her next Burlesque River story.

Connect with Kitty:
website: kittybardot.net
instagram: @ktbardot
twitter: @KittyBardot
facebook: facebook.com/Kitty-Bardot-312641412082507

www.BOROUGHSPUBLISHINGGROUP.com

If you enjoyed this book, please write a review. Our authors appreciate the feedback, and it helps future readers find books they love. We welcome your comments and invite you to send them to info@boroughspublishinggroup.com. Follow us on Facebook, Twitter and Instagram, and be sure to sign up for our newsletter for surprises and new releases from your favorite authors.

Are you an aspiring writer? Check out www.boroughspublishinggroup.com/submit and see if we can help you make your dreams come true.

Made in the USA
Middletown, DE
12 May 2021